Caught for Christmas

Skye Warren

I'll be home for Christmas...

The plan is simple. Break into the club and steal the money I need to save my father. The ex-military bouncer isn't going to stop me, even if he is hot as hell.

If only in my dreams...

Except he has a curious knack for knowing my next step.

And there's something dark underneath his desire, something dangerous. If he catches me, he might not let me go.

✧   ✧   ✧

CAUGHT FOR CHRISTMAS is a standalone holiday romance set in the sexy, suspenseful Stripped series.

Books in the Stripped series

PRAISE FOR THE STRIPPED SERIES

"Very Angsty 5 Star Read! This book is so compelling, you won't be able to put it down, this is one of those books that you'll want to save to re-read."

—Melissa, Books Can Take You There

"There's one thing I can say with certainty, Skye Warren never fails to deliver a heartfelt, slightly dark, I can't stop turning the pages story. This one is no different."

—Di, Twisted Sisters

"It's dark, mysterious, sexy, and I loved every page of it! There were twists and turns that I never saw coming! I love when an author is able to keep me guessing until the very end of the book."

—Book Fancy Book Blog

"The writing is so incredibly fluid, the characters so intriguing, and the story so captivating. If I could give this book more than five stars, I would. It's as emotional as it is sexy, and beautiful as it is dark. Absolutely flawless."

—Sammy, Just Let Me Read

Chapter One

Y OU KNOW THAT feeling of unadulterated bliss when you take your bra off at the end of a long day? Yeah, multiply that by a thousand when you factor in four-inch heels and a glitter thong. It's scratching the shit out of me underneath the trench coat I'm wearing, and it's my own damn fault.

I could have changed in the dressing room like the other girls, but I feel weird about it. I'm not really comfortable with other women. It's still too foreign. My childhood wasn't really tree houses and friendship bracelets. More like hideouts and cuffs if you were stupid enough to get caught.

Shaking my ass for random strangers? I can do that.

Changing clothes in the dressing room, filled with girls who will judge me and hate me? No, thanks. I've been to high school already. Almost twenty of them, actually, considering how much we moved around.

So I'm taking a walk in the cool, damp night instead. The wind gusts into places that are usually dry. Tanglewood is far enough south that we don't usually see snow, but tonight is especially cold. I'm looking forward to peeling this costume off my tired body and stepping into a hot shower.

"How much for the night?" a bum shouts from a darkened doorway.

"More than you got," I call back without slowing my stride.

"Amen," comes his fading response.

The streets are still pretty busy for the small morning hours, but I don't fool myself that I'm safe.

I spot a group of businessmen leaving a restaurant, hands clapped on shoulders, drunken hails for a flurry of cabs. The sushi restaurant is decked out in garland and lights. These guys would have no problem at all springing for a goddamn burger. They probably blew eight hundred dollars on tiny cups of sake already.

My body needs something other than breathing room. I can hear the rumble of my stomach over the engines and city sounds from the street.

I shove my hands into my coat pockets. *Don't ask for trouble, Bee. You're in enough trouble already.*

There are two packs of ramen noodles on my counter and an endless supply of water from the tap, but I would really love something hot and cheesy and full of carbs. It's the kind of meal I wouldn't hesitate to buy myself when I started dancing, knowing I'd work off more calories than I can eat. That's still true, but these days even a fifteen-dollar diner check is stretching the bounds of my wallet. My paycheck is generous. It's more than enough—if I didn't have to pay an old debt. Someone else's debt.

I'm two feet away from the men when my hands come out of my pockets. I feel them moving with a kind of muscle memory, bile rising in my throat at what I'm about to do. *They're just a bunch of rich bastards. They don't give a fuck about anyone but themselves. You'll be doing them a favor, stealing from them, bringing them down a notch.*

That's what Maisie would tell me, but what does she know? She's the reason I'm in this mess.

There's only the slightest jostle, the faintest tug of fabric. Then the wallet's in my pocket, not his.

He won't even think I took it. He'll head back into the restaurant to check the table first.

Poor rich bastard. I'm the one who doesn't care about anyone but myself.

I walk for five blocks, past where I would normally turn off. When the coast looks clear, I duck into a dark alley and check my haul. I'm not going to bother with the credit cards or ID. All I want is cash, and I find two crisp hundred-dollar bills and a few random twenties and tens.

Jackpot.

I fold them into my bustier through the lapels of my coat and toss the wallet into the dumpster. This means dinner tonight and a few more hot, melty meals besides. They won't scratch the surface of the larger debt, but my goals are small now. Something buttery with a hint of garlic.

A hand lands on my shoulder.

My heart knocks against my ribs, and I whirl to face my attacker. There are a lot of people who might have followed me in here. The guy whose wallet I stole. Or just some random asshole who wants to take what I won't give him. I'm prepared for a fight.

I'm not prepared for West.

His dark skin blends into the shadows, highlighting his eyes and the white of his teeth when he speaks. "What the fuck, Bianca?"

His shock mirrors mine. How did he follow me without me noticing? He must have kept pace from the club. I'm losing my touch, and at the worst possible time. "Can I help you?" I say coolly, stalling for time.

He rolls his eyes and reaches for me. I have a second's panic as his hand comes closer—is he going to hurt me? Is he going to *touch* me? Then his long fingers pluck the thin wad of cash from my bustier. He holds it up to the faint light. Somehow he managed to do that almost without touching my skin.

That can't be disappointment I feel, can it?

"Stealing," he says flatly.

I hate the judgment in his tone, the censure. "What's it to you?"

"Why do you need this?" he counters. "I know what dancers make at the Grand. And I know where you live. You can afford better than that."

My eyes narrow. "How the hell do you know where I live?"

"I've read the security profiles on all employees at the

Grand," he answers smoothly. Which isn't a bad excuse, since the security company does pretty intense workups. He ruins the innocent act by adding, "I've also followed you home a couple times."

It bothers me that he followed me home, but it bothers me way more that I didn't notice. "Looking for a little side action? I didn't know you were into that, Boy Scout."

West is a bouncer at the Grand, the club where I work. The girls call him *Boy Scout* because he never looks at us wrong, never asks for a private dance. He's a total gentleman, and exactly the kind of trouble I don't need.

"I'm worried about you," he says, his voice strangely honest, the kind of earnest I almost didn't know existed until I met him. He's naive, right? Way too gullible. I just hate how it makes my heart tug.

"Don't be," I tell him, snatching the wad of cash from his hand. "I can take care of myself."

He leans back just a fraction, and I get the feeling he's inspecting me. Whatever he sees, I doubt he's impressed. He works for Candy, who owns the Grand after Ivan gave it to her, and she has a gorgeous body. Hell, all the dancers have gorgeous bodies.

Meanwhile I'm too tired, too thin. Months of ramen noodles will do that to a girl. I can keep dancing, though, keep moving—muscle memory and all that. The same way I stole that wallet.

"Let me take you to dinner," he says.

My heart gives another kick, and I know this time it

isn't from fear. I nod toward the blue-glow horizon, skyscrapers like snow-capped mountains. It's already morning. "A little late for that."

"I'm still hungry," he says, his voice low—and seductive? I'm not sure what makes me think that, except that I'm feeling a little seduced. The wetness in dark places has nothing to do with windswept rain.

And that makes him dangerous. "No, thanks."

He pauses, not seeming particularly let down. He seems thoughtful instead—as if I'm a puzzle he's trying to figure out. "I know this great little Italian place. They stay open late as long as there's customers. And there's always customers."

Italian, huh? I bet they have lots of things that are cheesy and hot and—

Damn it, no.

"They bring you a basket of garlic bread to start," he continues like a goddamn sex-phone operator, and I'm paying by the minute. And why shouldn't I listen? I put on a show every night. "Fresh from the oven, with the butter browned around the crust. Sometimes I can get full just off the bread, but that's a shame."

My mouth is completely dry. "It is?"

"It is, because the fried calamari is the best I've ever had. Crispy and salty. You'll be licking your fingers afterward. I know I will."

A sound escapes me, something like a moan. I'm too damn hungry to be embarrassed about it. "Then what?"

"Well, that's just the appetizer. For the main course

there's so much to choose from. I've been there so many times but I don't think I've tried them all. There's the lasagna with the filling that's so creamy one forkful will fill you up. Then there's the Tuscan filet, cooked to order. But I think the best dish I've had there—"

My mouth isn't dry anymore. It's watering. I'm literally salivating at what he's describing, and he knows it. How does he know this about me? Why does he care? The cash slips from my fingers and falls to the damp alley ground, and I don't even care. I don't want the cash. I don't want to be a thief. I just want him to take me on a date to this place and never let it end.

"Tell me," I whisper.

He steps close, and I realize he's backed me up against the wall. There's nowhere to go from here, nothing to do as his long body presses against mine. I'm tall any day of the week, and especially with my stilettos. He's even taller, towering over me, his strong body both a shield and a cage against the wind. I'm about to combust from what he's describing, and the nearness of his body is the strike of a match.

His warm breath ghosts over my forehead. "The best dish is the gnocchi, each piece hand rolled, thick and stuffed with mozzarella they get straight from the farmer. There's this brown-butter sauce that—"

"No," I say, pushing him away. For a second my hands don't move him at all, his body way too strong to budge, and I panic. Old fear rises up in my throat, and my hands clench into fists.

Then he straightens and steps away, hands up as if to calm me.

I couldn't move him by force, only by words. By asking him to.

"No," I say again, a reminder for him—and for myself. I want him too much. And I can't have him. Not when I'm about to break through the security systems made by the company he works for. Not when I'm about to steal from his boss.

It will be a little like stealing from West.

Then I turn and run through the streets, my breath ragged and gasping as I sob out a denial—to myself, to him—leaving the money on the ground at his feet. He doesn't follow me this time, and I make it back to my crappy apartment and the packets of ramen noodles.

This is the world I'm living in now, the one I'm forced to inhabit. And all he offered me today, both the dinner and his earnest concern, are like the high heels and the glitter thong. Temporary. A means to an end. I take them off, feeling mostly relief. Relief and a little bit of regret.

CHAPTER TWO

B *ANG. BANG. BANG.*

I wake up on a gasp, sweat drenching my body. I push back damp hair and check the clock. It's seven o'clock in the morning, which means I've been sleeping for oh, about half a second.

No rest for the wicked, I guess.

Another round of raucous knocking at the door is joined by the angry stomps of my upstairs neighbor. "Sorry," I mutter, pushing the comforter off my legs and standing. The cold immediately settles into my bones, the air in here probably colder than outside.

I take a detour to the kitchen and grab a knife, because West was right. My apartment is not safe, and not only because of the location.

"Who is it?" I yell through the heavy door. The peephole was cracked to hell when I moved in—by an angry ex-boyfriend with a baseball bat, the landlord told me.

"It's Maisie." My mother.

I use my foot to push the chair away from the door and unlock the dead bolt. A girl can't be too careful, especially when there are mobster types who think I have their money.

Maisie holds up a white paper bag gone translucent with grease. "I brought breakfast."

I step back to let her inside, my stomach growling, my whole body tight with hunger. It doesn't want whatever dollar taco is in that bag. It wants gnocchi and garlic bread. It wants West.

She slides two hot dogs in cardboard containers onto the counter, the meat shiny and brown. "Voila."

I make a face. "Are those from yesterday?"

"Don't get picky," she says, sliding one over to me and taking the other for herself. "We have bigger problems to worry about."

Dread sinks in my empty stomach. "Jeb?"

I've called my parents Maisie and Jeb for as long as I can remember. They're more like an aunt and uncle who sweep in on a whirlwind with greasy food and cheap presents—and then leave when they're ready to go back to their own lives. We've spent more Christmases apart than together. I'm eighteen now, so the state thinks I'm old enough to take care of myself. The truth is I've been doing that since I turned twelve.

Maisie looks down, but not before a rare flash of emotion crosses her petite features. "They took him."

I stand up, shoving the stale hot dog away. "You said we had until next week."

Her face is pale, matching the white-blonde hair I inherited from her. "They moved up the timetable."

"Christ." I run my hands over my face, trying to

wipe away the exhaustion. It takes a long time to set up a con this big. Next week was already pushing it. "Why didn't you tell me about this mess sooner? Maybe we could have worked out a payment plan or, hell, I don't know."

She hesitates. "We didn't want to scare you."

"You didn't want to scare me," I repeat dully. I'd told them I wanted to go straight. I'd *told* them I'd never steal from the Grand, when they'd first suggested it months ago. Then they'd showed up last week, cowed and terrified—and I'd had to help. "You need me to steal fifty thousand dollars from my dangerous, violent boss or Jeb's fingers will get cut off. I think we're past being scared."

She bites her lip, giving me the pouty look that has gotten her out of so many tight spots. Well, that and her body. Jeb and Maisie are both good-looking, and they don't consider anything done in pursuit of a con to be cheating. "We knew you'd get mad," she said, her eyes going wide.

I hate that I look so much like her. I used that same look on the customers at the Grand to milk them out of their money. It's nothing like what she does, though. They gave me their money fair and square. Maisie only ever lies and steals.

"Who took him, Maisie?" I know they owe money to *someone,* but not who. "You need to tell me."

They've been cagey about the whole thing. Of course, that's standard operating procedure for Jeb and

Maisie. Still, I didn't expected Jeb to be abducted over this—and not so fast.

We should have had more time.

She sighs, her eyes falling shut. "The Caivano family."

"The mob? You stole money from the goddamn mafia?" God, no wonder Maisie and Jeb are terrified. The Caivano family isn't likely to work out a payment plan.

Her voice takes on a whining quality. "I knew you'd get angry."

"Oh no. Don't try to turn this around. You stole fifty thousand dollars from the mafia. And they aren't just going to cut off a finger, are they?"

The fear in her eyes proves my point. "They have him, Bee."

"They're going to kill him. And then they're going to kill you. And then they're going to kill me for being related to you, along with anyone else you've ever spoken to or known."

She shivers, and at least now I know she understands the situation. She understood it before she knocked on my door. She understood it when she stole these day-old hot dogs, but hell. This is all she knows how to do. Smile and pout and wheedle her way to getting what she wants.

Trade up. That's what she used to tell me. Other parents taught their kids to tell the truth, to be nice. Maisie taught me that the only thing that matters is trading up, even if you piss off some of the most dangerous men in the city.

Even if it means betraying people who trust me.

Her hands turn palm up, helpless. "Now you understand why we needed you to do the job."

The job. Bitterness is sharp on my tongue. This job that will cost me my job. More than that, it will cost me people I'd begun to think of as friends. *It will cost me West.*

"I told you I'll do it."

"We have to do it now."

She says *we,* but of course she means that I have to do it now. Not her. "When then?"

"The night after tomorrow."

An incredulous laugh bursts out of me. "Christmas Eve?"

I'm not sure why I thought that would be sacred to her when nothing else is.

She looks earnest. "The club will be closed. We have to do it soon."

I shake my head, frustrated. "It's *too* soon. We aren't even sure we can get into the security system. We haven't worked out all the kinks and—"

"We don't have a choice." She takes my hand, her blue eyes startling in their honesty. I've never seen her this focused on me before, not in eighteen years as her daughter. She's the flighty one, while I had to negotiate with the landlord for an extension on our rent. Now she looks dead serious—and worried. "They said they'll kill him if we don't bring the money soon. They…they sent me this."

She pulls something from her pocket and sets it on the counter. I've seen that plain silver band before.

They once hocked my bike with the ribbons in the handles. They've gone for days without food. They've traded their last dime for a security code to use on the next score. They give up anything and everything in pursuit of the game, but I've never seen Jeb not wearing this ring.

Now it's on my cracked kitchen counter, tarnished and coated in dried blood.

My throat tightens at the threat contained in that small band of silver. It tightens further at the thought of stealing from Candy and Ivan. Candy, because I'd started to respect her, even like her. And Ivan, because everyone in the city knows well enough to fear him. Stealing from him is as bad as stealing from the Caivanos.

The only difference is that I won't get caught. I can't get caught.

CHAPTER THREE

THE SOUND OF laughter draws me into the dressing room. It's a foreign sound, but I can't help but smile along with them. The girls have gathered their chairs and stools in a circle around Amelie. Her tummy is just starting to show, and she stops dancing next week. She holds up a little onesie with a mustache on it that says, *Mommy's Little Man*. The group gives a chorus of *oohs* and *ahhs*.

There's a table set up near the door with gifts and a diaper pail for cash. I've been to a few of these baby showers in the time I've been working here. The tradition is to give both money—to help out the new mother—as well as something cute to open during the shower. Normally I would throw in a hundred bucks or more. I'm not even close to these girls, but babies are crazy expensive and I like the idea of pitching in. In some ways it's as close to a family as I've ever gotten.

Only, I don't have a hundred bucks.

Maisie took most of my last paycheck. She said she'd use it as a payment toward the debt—a gesture of good faith so they'd give us more time, though obviously that didn't work.

And West took the money from the wallet. Or hell, maybe he left it lying on the ground.

No, most likely he returned it to the rightful owner, along with the wallet. Bastard.

So I'm flat broke. I press my last five-dollar bill between my fingers, feeling my stomach turn over. Without glancing around, I toss the money inside the diaper pail. It's shameful, and not only because I'm contributing so little money. It's shameful because I know I'm going to do worse tomorrow night. I'm going to steal from this place. I'm going to betray their trust.

"Bianca!"

I jump at the sound of my name. It feels like everyone stops and turns to face me.

Amelie smiles and waves me toward her. "Don't put that on the table. I want to see."

Dumbly, I look down at the small package I'm holding. At least I could make this from the supplies in my apartment. I'm not sure I could have made myself show up empty-handed. "It's nothing," I manage to say. God, I wish no one was looking at me. "Just something I made."

"You made this?" Amelie looks excited, and I curse myself in my head. Why did I say that? I meant that it's small and probably not even pretty.

I try to back away while she rips into the tissue paper, but I'm trapped by people and baby clothes all around, forced to stand in the middle of the pile while my lame offering is exposed.

Amelie squeals as she pulls out the knitted hat—brown with little teddy bear ears. Cute, but it's not like it was my idea or anything. I saw it once on a kid in a fancy stroller that looked like it belonged in the space age. That hat probably came from some ritzy store that I couldn't afford. This hat I made myself. I enjoy knitting. It's something to do with my hands when my body is too sore and tired to move.

"This is *the* most adorable thing I've ever seen," Amelie says, sounding awed.

"It's amazing," Candy agrees. "I didn't know you could knit. You're so talented."

It makes me blush and stammer that their praise seems genuine. I'm not used to that. I'm not used to doing anything right, actually. I prefer to stay in the edges, in the shadows, so that my inevitable fuckups don't get witnessed by anyone else.

Everyone is witnessing this, though. The hat is getting passed around, with each person exclaiming over it and rubbing the yarn between their fingers.

"Do you take commissions?" Vivian asks. "I would *love* a scarf in this fabric."

I'm not sure what I even answer. Something that sounds like yes but really means no. The truth is I'm not even going to be around long enough to make anything. Once I do the job tomorrow, I'll have to run. That fact feels like acid on my skin. I would have loved to skip work today, but I couldn't risk raising suspicion.

Then Amelie is standing, and before I can back away,

she has her arms around me. It feels sweet—and painful, because I don't deserve her gratitude. I don't even deserve to be here.

I manage to extricate myself without causing a scene, and they're already moving on to some game involving baby bottles.

My stomach feels like it's going to claw its way out of my throat. Hunger? Okay, sure, but I already tossed my last five dollars into a diaper pail. Besides, as starving as I am, I'm not sure I could keep anything down.

I press my hand over my mouth and stumble out of the dressing room. I'm not even sure where I'll go since the Grand opens in an hour, but I have to get out of here.

My eyes are on the floor, head down—so I don't see the wall of masculinity in front of me until I slam into it. I know without looking that it's him. West.

And God, it's almost like I want to be caught by him. Like I want to be *seen* by him, because before I can remember to hide my eyes, I'm looking up. He can see the tears in my eyes.

Concern darkens his expression. "What's wrong?"

I can't even answer him. I can't speak. I brush past him—he lets me. The dank outside air feels like freedom, but I know it won't last for long. I'll have to go back to dance, and he'll be there. He'll be waiting.

CHAPTER FOUR

I LIKE DANCING because of how honest it is. Trading sex for money has been around for centuries. Since the beginning of time, really. Cavewomen who bared their breasts, their bodies would have learned how to trade that for food and protection and warmth. The practice is still around today, part of every relationship—the endless transaction of pleasure and survival.

Stripping just brings it out in the open, makes the equation a little simpler for everyone to understand. This much for a lap dance and that much for a private show. It's the opposite of a con because everyone knows what they're going to get.

And that's how I dance—sexual but also straightforward. Some people have called me emotionless. The ice queen. Oh, they're probably right, but it doesn't hurt my tips any.

Then Ivan gave the Grand to Candy, and she switched the place over to a burlesque theater. A little more flash, a little less flesh. The biggest difference is that I'm usually dancing with other girls. I have to admit, it's kind of nice. There's an energy to the group of us, a collective strength.

Then the song ends, and I'm alone again.

Up there I felt nothing but the burn of muscle and beat of music. Now I feel nothing but dread.

I trail the other girls down the hallway with track lighting on the floor.

A large body steps in front of me. My heart skips in fear before I recognize him. *West.* I'm not afraid of him, not in the way I am of most men. At least I know what they want from me, even if I have to worry that they might take it by force. West is looking for something different, and that scares me in a different way.

His eyes are dark with concern. "Is something wrong?"

I force myself to give him a cool smile. "Why would you think that?"

"Maybe because you're going to make yourself bleed."

My gaze flicks down, and I realize my fists are clenched tight, nails pressing into my palms. I open my hands, and white crescents remain in my flesh, bloodless and pained. So I haven't hidden my tension as much as I'd hoped.

That's dangerous. Dangerous because when they discover the club has been robbed, West will remember that I was nervous.

He'll know it was me.

I give him a sultry smile. "Nothing is wrong now that you're here."

He narrows his eyes, not fooled for an instant. He

tugs my hand, and then we're in the dark hallway behind the stage, hidden from view, even from each other. The music moves through us, some familiar Christmas tune, more feeling than sound. "You missed your last shift," he says.

My heart squeezes. I'd been trying to find some other way to come up with the cash. Any other way. So I staked out a local check-cashing shop to see if I could get the money that way. Their security was too tight, but the florist shop next door would easy as pie. I'd breeze right past those poinsettias and rich red roses to the register.

However, they wouldn't have nearly enough money on hand.

"I was busy," I say, walking my fingers up his broad, firm chest. "But I'm here now."

He isn't fooled by my misdirection, but he doesn't remove my hand either. That's something.

He closes his eyes, frustrated and something else. "I wish you'd tell me what's going on. I wish you'd let me help."

Oh sure, that would be great. *Please help me steal fifty thousand dollars from a man who would never stop hunting you down.* No, he's too much of a Boy Scout to steal a penny, no matter how much I need it. No matter how much he wants to do the dirty things his dark eyes promise.

"You can help me by taking me into a VIP room," I whisper, pressing my body close. Technically there's not supposed to be naughty business in those rooms since we're a burlesque show, but some girls still break the rules. I wouldn't mind breaking them, to throw him off my tracks.

Wouldn't mind the extra cash.

And I wouldn't mind getting up close and personal with him.

My hip brushes against something hard and thick. *Ooh, very nice.* I know that I'd be able to distract him in that room, Boy Scout or not.

His eyes glaze over, and I know he's contemplating what we could do in the VIP room.

"I'd make it good for you," I whisper.

He shakes his head as if clearing it. His hands grip my hips, pulling me in close. "No, Bianca. When you come for me, it won't be because you want to distract me. And it sure as hell won't be because I'm paying you."

I manage a laugh that sounds hollow to my own ears. "I didn't take you for a cheapskate."

His eyes sharpen. "Is that what you need? Money?"

My breath leaves me in a rush. He hit a little too close to home. I do need money, but I doubt my Boy Scout has a big stash of cash. Not after making shit money in the military for years. Ivan pays well, but he's only been here less than a year. Only illegal, shady shit like the things Maisie and Jeb are involved with could produce that kind of money.

I drop my voice. "You have no idea what I need."

His fingers tighten briefly on my hips, and surprise flares inside me. So the tamed wolf has spirit after all.

Heat forms between my legs, the suggestion whispering through me—what it would be like if he let go.

I force the thought away, because this can only be a means to an end.

"Bianca," he says, his voice thick. "Don't do this."

Panic flares, because he can't know what I'm going to do. Can he? There's no way he can know. He only means pushing him away. That's all. "I'm not doing anything. You're the one who can't stop being so damn…" So damn sweet. So damn sexy. God, I can't stand him. "So damn *good* all the time."

His lids lower. "Is that how you see me?"

"That's what you are. A Boy Scout."

His smile comes slow and almost lazy. "And you want to see how bad I can be?"

A shiver runs through my body. The truth is that I like him this way, honorable and kind.

I just know he's not made for me. He'd turn away from me if he knew all the things I'd done in my life, all the cons I've helped Maisie and Jeb pull off. It won't matter anyways, because whether West remembers my nervousness or not, whether he suspects me or not, I'll have to run. I can't stick around and risk Ivan finding me out once I've stolen from him.

Which means tonight is my last night at the Grand.

The last time I'll see West.

I let something drop—the pretense, the act. When I lean forward, it's just me. Bianca. No transaction, no trade. Just a gentle kiss of my lips to his, fleeting warmth, a promise unfulfilled.

"No," I whisper against his lips. "Don't change. I like who you are."

Then I turn and walk away, leaving him in the dimly lit hallway, the swing of my hips a silent goodbye.

CHAPTER FIVE

I T MAY SEEM weird that someone who had committed a felony by the time I turned six would like to knit. The truth is that I learned to pick locks using knitting needles—the circular ones are perfect for small pins and little hands. Plus, throw in some yarn and the whole thing looks innocent, even if your bag gets searched. Of course since then I've moved on to more elaborate picks and hooks, professional tools of the underground trade. But I always keep needles, and a skein of yarn, in my bag for luck.

I tighten my hold on the fraying leather straps, trying to get into the right headspace.

Except I can't get into the headspace where I'm cold and calculating.

All I can think about is West.

The Grand looms ahead, almost glowing against the pitch dark sky. It looks like a fortress, impenetrable. When I started working here a year ago, security was had been about big muscles, shiny guns, and a bad reputation. Very few people would have dared to steal from Ivan's pet business, and anyone too high to know better would learn their lesson quickly once his men found them.

Then someone threatened Candy, Ivan's favorite girl.

Now security is a lot tighter, with cameras covering every square inch and laser sensors on every door and window. But I'm constantly casing whatever place I'm in, always monitoring the entry points and exits. I find weak spots in their security system.

Old habits and all that.

Which is why I know exactly how to break into the Grand.

"Bee," comes a whisper from the alley. I meet Maisie in the shadows, where she slips me a folded piece of paper. "The code to the alarm."

Suspicion rises up in me. "Do I even want to know how you got this?"

"Of course not," she says as if she doesn't care. Because she doesn't. Whatever illegal or unethical thing she had to do doesn't matter. Whoever got hurt doesn't matter.

Trade up. All that matters is that she got what she wanted.

Right now I can't even blame her. Some very scary men have Jeb. They won't be treating him well. And if we don't get them their money, they won't ever let him go.

The paper is cool between my thumb and forefinger. "This means you can come in with me."

She shakes her head, a flash of white-blonde hair in the dark. "I'll stand guard. That was always the plan."

The plan had been for her to cut the alarm. I'd be ready to go inside the second the alarm went dead. And she would stand guard, because it didn't make sense for her to catch up. I'm the safe cracker in the family. Maisie has the smile, and Jeb has the charm. And me? I've had a good ear for clicks ever since I was a little girl.

Now that she doesn't need to cut the alarm, she could come in with me. And the fact that she doesn't want to has more to do with hedging her bets than keeping a lookout.

"Fine," I say, my teeth clenched. I tell myself for the millionth time that I won't be sucked into any of their schemes, but how can I even believe my own lies? The second they show up on my doorstep with some sob story—and some crazy violent assholes on their tail—I'm back to doing their bidding.

She puts her hand on my arm. "Bee, don't be upset. You need to go in calm. Clear your mind."

I close my eyes and squeeze them tight. I do need a clear mind if I'm going to crack that safe. "You'll be here when I get out?"

I hate how small my voice sounds, how childlike.

"Of course," she says in that carefree way. And I know better than to believe her.

It's something else that pulls me across the street, something else that makes me climb the metal gate. A sense of duty. Or maybe something darker. The fear that if I don't do this, if I turn my own parents away from my door, I'll have no one left.

The cameras sweep over the courtyard in an irregular pattern, but I've watched it. I've learned it. And I use that knowledge now to evade them, pausing behind the broken fountain before running across the broken cobblestones.

I don't bother trying to pick the fancy carbon locks. It only takes me a few minutes to pry apart hinges from old wood and wedge the door open from the other side.

That's the fatal flaw of this place. No matter how much high-tech security infrastructure you add, it's still an old building, a genial building, one designed to welcome people in—not keep them out.

The security system beeps in warning.

I enter the code on the slip of paper, and it goes silent.

Well, that was the easy part. Now I have to break into the basement, which will be no small feat. And then I have to break into a safe before anyone finds me. And then I'll have to get out of town.

I'll get out of town and never be able to come back.

The Grand is silent and still and almost pitch-black, only the placid green blinks from the security system to light the way. The energy is different now too, without the avid curiosity of the attendees, without the hard beauty of the girls. It feels truly grand, with old-world elegance and an air of demure calm.

It hurts to think about robbing this place, even while I'm halfway there. As if I'm defiling something pure. It hurts to think about leaving and never coming back.

Maisie is waiting for me outside. Jeb is waiting for me, his life hanging in the balance.

So I force myself to cross the floor and head to the hallway by the stage. There's a set of stairs leading down. I've only been down here once, when Ivan hired me. I never planned to rob the place, but I cased it anyway. So I could tell he kept the safe in his desk, bottom drawer. It would be something heavy, not something normally transportable. He would have had it built into the room, small and impenetrable.

I do have to pick the lock on the basement door. I bypass the half-made hat and the knitting needles in my bag and get the equipment I need. The hinges here are made of steel, the door itself a heavy metal as well. It takes me longer than I hope to get through the three dead bolts, each with a different size and shape bolt. I leave more scratches on the locks than I'm comfortable with. It's sloppy, but I don't have time to be neat. Every second that front door hangs open is a second I'm vulnerable.

I can't forget what's at stake here. Not just my life but Jeb's. And Maisie's. They wouldn't stop with him if they're trying to send a message. Their acts of violence are almost legendary. Everyone knows how ruthless they are. We don't stand a chance.

Finally I push the door open. The floor of the Grand had seemed dark, but it's nothing compared to the basement. There isn't even the thread of moonlight through high stained-glass windows or the green glow of security buttons. There's nothing at all.

I take two steps in the direction of the desk. I remember the placement of the room. There is no other furniture but that. And with the heavy safe built into it, he wouldn't have moved the desk.

Two more steps. It's disconcerting moving in the darkness, like I'm floating in a sky without stars.

A small scuffing sound makes me freeze.

The whistle of metal hinges makes the hair on my neck stand up. Then the door slams shut behind me. *I'm not alone.*

"Hello, Bianca."

CHAPTER SIX

THE VERY WORST thing isn't what will happen to me now. It isn't even what will happen to Jeb or Maisie, who got themselves into this mess. Who got *me* into this mess.

The worst thing is that it's West who's caught me.

I fought so hard against him, against my attraction to him and the strange trust I had for him. He's the one who's going to bring me down. But then, maybe I always knew he would. I pull the old leather bag in front of my like a shield, even though I know it's useless. I've been caught.

"How did you know?"

His lips firmed. "I didn't."

I let myself take stock of him, every muscled inch. His jaw is hard, more angular tonight. His skin is a beautiful darkness, as if he was born of the night itself. His body is strong, hanging back because he knows he doesn't have to force me to make me do what he wants. If I ran, he could catch me.

In his right hand is a gun. I always knew the bouncers of the Grand were packing heat, but it's a different thing to see the gun up close. He wouldn't use it on me, would he? But then I didn't think he'd suspect me either. I didn't think he'd *catch* me. And I can't afford to test him on this.

"You're waiting in a basement," I say, thankful my voice doesn't shake too much. "And you don't look surprised to see me. You must have known something."

He gives a hollow laugh. "That's why. You're always watching me. Always observing. And you made it clear it's not because you want to date me."

I want to date him more than anything, but I wouldn't even know how to date. It's not something you can do when you're constantly in between cons—not unless the boyfriend is a mark. "So I must have wanted to steal?"

He lifts one broad shoulder. "You've picked up extra shifts sometimes and then suddenly have to skip them. You've lost weight. You chipped in five dollars into the diaper pail."

Guilt stabs me at the reminder. "So?"

"You usually put in more."

I manage not to flinch, but barely. It hurts to know he saw me do that—and that he'd been watching me long enough to know what I usually do. It hurts to know he's seen me lose weight, as if I'm breaking apart right in front of him. "You caught me," I whisper.

His eyes soften just a fraction. "I made a guess. I hoped I'd be wrong."

My heart clenches. "I'm sorry."

"For what?"

For not being the girl you needed, a girl who would be good enough for you. "For proving you right."

His expression is grave, his hands almost gentle as he takes the bag from me. I hold tight for a second, a fleeting rebellion, before letting it go. I feel almost naked without it, exposed.

West nods toward the desk—and the wing-back chair behind it. "Have a seat, Bianca."

The chair is comfortable when I sink down into it, and I have no doubt it's expensive. But it might as well be a prison cell to me, the wide leather wings blocking me in as effectively as steel bars. Especially when I spot the duct tape sitting on the desk.

My eyes widen. "Wow, you came prepared. You really are a Boy Scout."

He gives a wry smile and sets the bag down against the wall. "Don't think that means I'm going to take it easy on you."

"Who are you going to call?" My voice is hoarse, exposing my weakness, but I have to know. "The cops? Or Ivan?"

"Neither," he says simply.

Shock is a cold rush from my heart to my toes. I know what some men in his position would do. Most men, really. They would take advantage. I'm about to be in a vulnerable position. I'll be at his mercy. He could touch me. He could fuck me. And no one would believe me—or even care.

I never thought he would do that to me. He

wouldn't…

Would he? I can't be sure.

The sound of duct tape ripping from the roll snaps my attention to him. He places it over my wrist, smoothing the silver tape along the butter-soft leather. *He's taping me to the chair.*

It's over my black long-sleeved T-shirt, but tight enough that I can't wriggle free.

He pulls another piece of tape out. "So what was it?" he asks almost conversationally. "Drugs? Gambling?"

My lips tighten. I hate for West to think of me like that, that I would have gotten myself into this mess. Maisie and Jeb are the ones crazy enough to steal from the fucking mafia.

But in another way I *did* get myself into this. I went along with this plan even though it was too soon.

Even though it's wrong.

Even though it's immoral and screws over the very people who have been my friends the past few months. That's why I'll never get to be with West, why I'll never deserve him. I could dream of his strong hands and whispered words. I could imagine my silver-blonde hair over his dark chocolate skin as I worked my way down his body. And that's all I'll ever have—those dirty-sweet dreams.

We would have been beautiful together.

I can't ruin him like this. "You don't want to do this," I whisper.

He smooths the last piece of tape over the chair,

locking me in. "Do what?"

"Touch me." He would hate himself after. He isn't that kind of man. I wasn't wrong about him. I may have pushed him into doing something drastic with my mixed signals and then breaking in here. But if he touches me like this, while I'm tied up, he'll only hate himself later.

A short laugh. "I want to do a lot more than touch you, Bianca. And I think I've earned that right, don't you?"

There's a lump in my throat. "Not like this. Not while I'm tied up."

Are you sure about that, Bee? Didn't you taunt him for being too good? Now he's offering to be bad. The voice in my head sounds too much like Maisie for comfort.

He runs a dark finger down my cheek. "There's no better time. Now you can't run away."

With every word, the room seems to shrink, the bonds seem to get tighter. The air seems to get sucked out of the basement. There's nothing here but me and him, floating in a black void. No escape.

My fists tighten, and I tug against the tape. Nothing happens. "You can't do this."

His smile is hard, but his words are gentle. "How are you going to stop me?"

"West, please." I don't know why I'm fighting so hard, why I'm near tears. I never expected him to take advantage of me. I'm supposed to be tougher than this. I've been messed with on a con before. I know how to endure things. But it's worse with him.

"And you know what else?" he asks, studying me. "I think you'll like it."

My body grows warm—humiliation? Fear? There's something else too. Something hot and sensual, because I want West. I've always wanted him. And now it looks like I'll have him.

He stands and pulls his phone out. "It's me. Send it down."

CHAPTER SEVEN

S HOCK RENDERS ME speechless. What is he having sent down? I could have been okay with what he did to me. Maybe. I would have been okay with him touching me if we'd been in a bed, both of us hot and willing. Being tied up turns me on, but it also makes my heart twist in fear. I don't want him to be this man. I want him to be better than that, just like he believed I was better than a common thief.

If he's bringing down some other men to touch me, to use me, I won't be able to endure that. Not the pain of their hands or cocks. Especially not the knowledge that it was *West* who forced this on me.

My teeth are pressed together so hard, my whole body clenched tight against what might happen next. Tears burn their way down my cheeks. *No no no.*

"Wait," I say, close to begging. And then I am begging, whispering for him to *stop please no.*

His expression turns soft with sympathy—the kind of implacable sympathy that means he's going to do it anyway. He runs a hand over my head, pushing the black beanie off and stroking my hair. "It's as soft as I thought it would be," he says, almost to himself. "Softer. Like silk."

There's a knock from the basement door, and then someone pushes it open. I can hear footsteps coming down the steps. Only one person as far as I can tell, but maybe there are more. Anyone other than West would be too much. *Oh God.*

Someone reaches the bottom step and then comes into view.

My heart gives a hard, angry kick. It's Blue. He owns the security company the Grand uses. I know that he and West used to be in the military together, and sure enough, they clasp hands briefly in a gesture of masculine intimacy that makes my stomach pitch.

Blue doesn't look surprised to see me. He studies me, his expression unreadable. "She looks worried."

"She should be," West says, his response fast and easy. That's how they're taking this, without shock or drama. Just a girl caught in their web, something to be eaten.

Except that Blue is in a relationship with Hannah, one of the girls who used to work here. He wouldn't fuck with me, would he? Not when he has a girl he's into at home. But then I know as well as any girl here that commitment doesn't mean much to a lot of men. When they come to the club, they don't see us as women, as girlfriend material. We're just warm bodies to grab and to fuck before they go home to the real women in their lives.

Blue sighs. "Are you sure about this? We'd get in serious trouble if Ivan finds out."

Well, that's a surprise. And a relief. Ivan will be mad if they touch me? I hadn't figured he'd care, but I'll use any excuse to get out of this now.

West shakes his head, firm. "I'm handling this my way."

There's a long pause while Blue considers me. "You know I owe you one," he says finally. "Or two or three."

My heart sinks. Any hope I had dies a quick death. He's going to let this happen.

West smiles faintly. "That's because you're a crazy fucker. Always getting yourself into trouble."

"And you have my back every fucking time."

"Yeah," West says, voice soft. "And you have mine."

The moment would be touching if I wasn't terrified of what they were going to do to me. "I'm sorry," I burst out. "I got—I got in over my head with something. I wasn't going to take a lot. I would have put it back."

That's only kind of a lie. I had some vague plans to send the money back, but it would have taken me forever to earn that much.

Blue barely spares me a glance. "Do you want me to stick around?"

West laughs. "Like the old days? You always did like to watch."

"Not anymore. Not since Hannah. Speaking of which, she'd kick my ass if she found out I let you do this. She'd kick your ass too."

"I don't doubt it," West says, but he doesn't sound

concerned. "Give her my best."

"Will do."

Then Blue hands something over to West—a big white paper bag—and turns to leave. Just like any ordinary day, they're nodding their goodbyes and turning away. As if I'm not tied up here.

"No, wait. Don't leave me here." I'm desperate enough to press any advantage. "Hannah would hate this. It isn't right. She'll find out and she'll—"

Blue just shakes his head, waving away my plea. "Don't look at me. I wanted to do a lot worse than he's planning."

That shuts me up quick. Then he's gone up the stairs, leaving me alone with West and whatever he's got in that white paper bag.

CHAPTER EIGHT

H E SETS THE bag down on the desk with a small but solid *thud.* It has weight, whatever is inside. I've seen a lot in eighteen years, and my mind can imagine horrible things.

Whips, chains.

Chemicals to wipe away any trace of blood.

What can I say? My parents know some unsavory people.

But when he cracks open the bag, just a smidge, I know it's something else entirely. It doesn't smell like ammonia or chlorine. It smells like garlic and onions and butter. The inside of the bag is lined with foil—I can see that from here. That must be how it kept those delicious smells inside. Now that he's opened the top, the savory scent of fresh bread and melted cheese fill the basement.

My mouth waters. Is this how he's going to break me down? I have visions of him eating in front of me, bite after bite, never letting me have a taste. Torture. "What are you going to do with that?"

He looks amused now. "You are the least trusting person I know." His smile fades. "There's probably a good reason for that."

My stomach grumbles. Loudly. I can't help but blush. It's embarrassing to be in this position—tied up and so obviously starving. "Maybe I would be more trusting if you told me what you planned to do with me."

He turns to rifle through the bag, taking out black plastic containers and foil-wrapped packages. There are utensils and a couple bottles of water. It's like a romantic picnic—except I'm tied up and he's holding my life in his hands.

"I was thinking you could eat," he says. "To begin with. You look like a stiff wind could knock you over. There's only so long instant noodles can hold a person up."

"How do you know what I've been eating?" I stiffen in the soft leather chair, suspicious. "Have you been in my apartment?"

He raises one eyebrow. "Jesus, woman. It was an exaggeration. At least I thought it was. If I'd known you were living on instant noodles, I probably *would* have been in your apartment, doing this before now."

Great, so I'm actually a cliché of a hungry person. "You know that's still breaking and entering, right? Even if you're only doing it to bring me food."

"You're really going to talk to me about breaking and entering?"

Fair point. "Well, I wouldn't have appreciated it then, and I don't appreciate it now."

He smiles, a little mischievous and somehow shy.

"That's because you haven't tasted this vodka cream sauce. I have a feeling you'll be singing a whole different tune then."

My stomach clenches hard at the thought, and I'm afraid he might be right. I'm so hungry, both for food and for someone who gives a damn. He's standing in front of me, offering them both.

It's just a mirage though. When I drag myself through the sand to get to him, I'll find he was never really there. What future can there be for us? At some point he'll have to turn me in. He can't let me break in and go free. He's too much of a Boy Scout for that.

His gun is sitting beside the bag, and it's a painful contrast. The way he's taking care of me and the way he's threatened me. The hard soldier and the man who could have been my boyfriend.

He pulls out an aluminum container and opens it, revealing stuffed pasta in a cream sauce. Another package reveals a jumble of glistening garlic bread, studded with golden-white flecks of garlic and green herbs. His strong hands rip a piece of the bread and dip it into the sauce.

Then he holds it up to my mouth.

It smells delicious, almost painfully good, and my stomach caves in on itself in anticipation.

I force myself to wait, though, because I'm used to denial. I'm used to wanting. "You could use a fork," I say, my voice only a little unsteady.

"I could," he says, "but I like it better this way. I'm hoping you'll trust me a little more if I'm the hand that feeds you."

"Very funny," I say darkly.

"Who's laughing?" he counters, pressing the food to my lips, making them wet and slick with cream.

I can't ignore it any longer. I can't deny myself what I want—what I need. I open my lips, and he presses the bread inside. It's like rapture on my tongue, a burst of salty flavor that resounds through my entire body. A moan escapes me, long and low, and I actually clench my thighs from the sensual force of it.

His fingers follow the food, his calloused flesh a contrast to the soft bread. He slides them along my lips before pulling out again. His eyes are dark, and I know he's hard as a rock behind his jeans.

I swallow and beg him with my eyes for another bite. He's already ripping off another piece, already dipping it in the cream. We perform again without a word, his offering at my lips, my acceptance and his entry. He touches me again, finger pad over my tongue, and this time I moan for a different reason.

I swallow again, knowing that I'll follow him anywhere tonight. "What happens after this?"

He looks down at his hands. In a slow, deliberate motion he brings his forefinger to his mouth and sucks it clean. The motion is straightforward, the way someone might lick a crumb off their own finger. Except there's nothing there except a lingering taste from my mouth. It's like he's kissing me, tonguing me, without even touching me, and I feel the sensation to my core.

"Then it will be my turn," he says.

CHAPTER NINE

HE OPENS MORE containers and feeds me lasagna and gnocchi and braciole that falls apart in my mouth. There's enough food here to feed me for a week or maybe longer, but he's only giving me bites of each dish. My stomach has tightened from a month without much food, and I fill up quickly. He seems to notice that, and he reaches for one black container he had set aside.

Inside is a layered cake, rich brown on the bottom and lighter layers of cream on top. Without a word he spears a fork inside and holds it up for me to eat. Chocolate sweetness bursts on my tongue, and I think my eyes roll to the back of my head. It's too much pleasure, too much goodness.

A soft sigh escapes me, along with the question I've been holding in. "Why?"

"Why what?" His eyes are dark, and I know exactly why. This thing between us has turned sexual. Or maybe it was sexual all along. When he tied me up, when he waited for me in the dark.

All of it was leading to this.

My voice is low, a side effect of the decadence, the richness he's been feeding me. "You could do anything you want to me. Why this?"

"I'm not a martyr, if that's what you think. I'm doing this because it turns me on. Just looking at you turns me on, hearing your breathy little moans turns me on, touching you turns me on."

My throat is suddenly dry, and I swallow. "And then?"

"I'm not done with you, Bianca." It's like he's making a vow. "I haven't even started."

A shiver runs through me, and I force myself to meet his gaze. He promises so much in that one look. Pleasure. Fulfillment. He promises a future, and that's how I know it's a lie.

And strangely enough, that's how I can trust it. I know all about lies. I grew up with them. I survive on them. It was that awful earnestness that I couldn't handle, when he thought I might have been a different girl, a better girl—when he might have believed in me. Now he knows the truth about me. There can be no future. Only this.

"Then start," I whisper.

He was waiting for that—for desire, for permission. I know, because he doesn't wait any longer. As soon as the word is out of my mouth, he dips his finger into the top layers of cream and presses it into my mouth. He isn't hesitant. He doesn't wait for me to let him in. He just pushes his finger inside, smearing heaven on my tongue.

Then he's leaning down, his face inches from mine. I can feel his heat, his breath.

His mouth closes over mine, hard and demanding. This isn't a gentle kiss. It isn't a question.

It's a promise, just like the look in his eyes. He tastes the chocolate cream, and he tastes me with equal fervor, tilting my head back so I'm trapped against the chair. His hand cups my jaw, tilting me up to open to him, to surrender completely.

It feels as good as I always dreamed. Before I even knew West, when he was just some fantasy of a man who cared. He pleasures me, using his tongue to tease me and taunt me. And at the same time, he possesses me, claiming me with every press of his lips and stroke of his thumb against my cheek. I'm surrounded by him. Everything that came before—the savory meal and the sweet dessert only built to this moment, when I'm tasting him for the first time.

There's something specific about the way he kisses me, the movement of his tongue, the rhythm he uses. It feels like sex, like he's already fucking me even though we both have our clothes on. I squirm in the seat, pressing my legs together to assuage the ache.

He notices, pulling back. His lids are low. "You hungry, sweetheart?"

He doesn't mean for food.

I can only nod. *Please.*

His lips curve in a lazy smile. "Me too."

He bends and kisses me again, and I'm lost to his mouth, his uniquely male taste. Only vaguely do I feel him touching me over my arms and down my sides. And then sudden warmth of large hands cupping my breasts. I gasp, but he's already gone, already moving downward, tracing a path over my body.

One hand slips beneath the band of my soft black pants. The touch of two fingers against my sex makes me jolt against the tape, but my wrists are still bound to the chair.

"Shh," he soothes against my mouth. "You want this, baby. I can feel how wet you are."

I whimper, squirming in my seat, pressing myself farther away—and then pushing right up against his hand in shameless need. "Don't make me wait."

It's the worst kind of torture, feeling his strong hand hold very still. It's like he's punishing me for refusing him, and I can only rock against his hand in rhythmic plea.

"We're done waiting," he says softly.

He pulls his hand away and stands.

CHAPTER TEN

"**W**AIT. NO." IT was one thing when I thought he was going to fuck me. I've had men fuck me before. If they're gentle enough, I might have even enjoyed it.

What West is doing with his head between my legs is something different. Something sweeter.

"What's wrong?" His eyes meet mine, and I can see the hunger in them. He doesn't want the food from the restaurant, though. He wants me. My body, which is spread open to him, already wet.

"I don't do this." My voice is too high-pitched. *Too scared.*

A rough laugh. "You don't have to do anything. I'm going to do all the work, baby."

In another life that's what this tape and this chair could have meant: letting him do all the work. Relaxing enough to give him control. But we aren't in that world, where I'd have a choice. It's a luxury—choice—and I've spent my whole life backed up against the wall, hungry and desperate and fighting to survive.

"Don't," I whisper.

He frames my core with his large hands, pushing my

thighs apart. His eyes are almost black as they stare at my sex. "I have a feeling I'm never going to see you after today, whether I taste you or not. And I really fucking want to taste you."

The words wash over me, and it feels like relief. I don't really want him to stop, but I'm afraid. Afraid of what he means when he says we won't see each other again. Because he'll turn me over to the cops? Because he'll turn me over to Ivan?

Or because he's thinking of letting me go? My heart pounds at the thought. And he knows I'll run far away if he does.

"You're too much of a Boy Scout," I say, and even I can hear the challenge in my voice. I want him to prove me wrong, even though it seems almost impossible. How can he change who he is?

How could I have been wrong about him?

His expression is severe. "A fucking Boy Scout. I spent years in the fucking desert, where even looking at a woman wrong could mean her life was over. So I didn't. I wasn't a monk. I had hookups when I was on leave. What did it get me, Bianca? What's the fucking point?"

It rips me apart to hear him questioning this. As much as I want him to touch me, to ignore my protests, I would hate it too. I love him being a Boy Scout. Love the honorable man that he is, his mouth inches from my bare pussy—but he won't lean in. He just won't, and it's killing him.

My hands grab onto the chair, holding myself steady.

"Taste me, West. Touch me."

His eyes are hooded. I know he thinks this is about what he just said—and it is, but not how he thinks. I don't pity him. The man is kind and handsome as hell. He could score with any girl he sees right now. But he wants me. He wants this. And it's a kind of honor to be able to give it to him.

And no matter that he questions my motives, he doesn't wait. He has what he needed: permission.

His head lowers, and he places a kiss on my mound—a chaste kiss only. I feel the heat of it sear me. He touches me everywhere, his hands on my thighs, his torso between my legs, his lips on my sex.

He flicks a glance at me, and I see in it all the banked desire. He's been waiting longer than one night for this. Longer than the few months we've worked here together. It's like he's been waiting forever for this, and I feel that even stronger when he returns for an openmouthed kiss against my pussy.

He kisses me like he's starved for me, tongue digging deep, licking every drop of arousal, teeth scraping gently over tender, swollen flesh.

The basement had been quiet before, but now it's a riot of sounds. My whimpers and moans, incoherent, babbling. His soft words of praise, murmured against my skin, telling me how beautiful I am, how good I taste— how long he's wanted me.

He pushes two fingers inside me, and they slide in easily. I'm so slick from what he's doing, his tongue on my clit and the scruff of a late-night shadow against my mound.

His other hand tightens on my thigh as he fingers me, and I know he's imagining his cock inside me, how I'd feel tightening around him. I'm imagining it too. I squeeze his fingers instead, and it's a tease for us both.

"Fuck," he mutters under his breath.

I moan and push my hips against his face, begging for more.

He gives it to me, sucking directly on my clit—and it feels like lightning sparking through my body, sparking at my core and radiating out. The orgasm takes me by surprise, my entire body shaking and jerking against the bonds. I'm held by the chair and the tape, but also his hands and his mouth. I shudder in the small space of freedom I have, rocking against the walls that hold me, pushing against them even as I never want to leave.

It's only then, as the aftershocks of the orgasm shiver through me, that I feel the tape on my right-hand side loosen and come undone.

CHAPTER ELEVEN

THERE'S NOTHING MORE honest than the moment of climax, the pure pleasure of it, the surrender. And afterward there's an intimacy that you can't escape. That's what makes the moment uncomfortable for people who don't care about each other. It's what makes the moment poignant now, when West pulls back, his expression still taut with arousal—and a supremely male satisfaction after making me come.

I have to force myself not to feel it too deeply, not to want him too much.

I have to force myself not to show that my hand is loose.

If I pulled away now, he would hear the tape. He would see my arm swing free. And he'd be close enough to restrain me physically. I need to wait until he's distracted, and physically farther away, like when he spoke to Blue earlier. Then I can grab the gun on the desk and escape.

He's about to stand. I see the muscles in his arm flex. I feel the rush of cool air as it sweeps between our bodies.

"Wait." A few minutes ago I said this to make him stop. Now I don't want him to stop. Stopping means I'll have to fight my way free. It means our moments in the dark will end.

One eyebrow rises. His lids are still low, his full lips damp with my cream. "Baby?"

Just that one word turns me inside out, the lazy way he speaks it, the sexy confidence.

"What about you?" I ask in a rush, clinging to any excuse. Clinging to him.

"What about me?"

"Let me touch you. Let me…please you."

His expression turns stark. "Ah fuck, there's nothing I want more. But it wouldn't be right. Not like this."

I knew he was a Boy Scout underneath all that sexy swagger. "So you can get me off, but I can't get you off? That doesn't seem fair?"

A smile plays at his lips. "None of this is fair. I want you in my bed, not in Ivan's office. I want you free and clear." The smile fades. "But I don't have that."

Panic claws at my throat. However much he wanted to taste me, that's how much I want to taste him. It's not about salt or about sex. It's about giving him pleasure. It's about that poignant moment right after.

"Please," I whisper.

He tenses. "Oh shit, baby. We can't. Not like this."

Then we would never do it, and that thought fills me with despair. If I can get free, he'll never see me again— just like he thought. "I know it's not right, West. I know it's not ideal. But this is how it happened. This is all we have."

54

He may not like the way it happens, but he's a soldier at heart. He understands working with what you have. He understands survival too.

"Christ, baby." His eyes almost glaze over, his expression so tense it's as if he's climaxing. He even presses a hand to his jeans, pushing himself roughly, almost punishing himself for being so turned on.

I keep going, desperate now. There's only one thing I can bargain with, and it's the truth. "I wanted you all along. I was lying to you before. Lying to myself. I wanted everything you had to offer, but I was afraid. And then there was this debt. And I'm telling the truth that I didn't want to do this, I *hated* to do this, because you would find out about it."

My throat closes up, and I know I was too honest. I went too far, and he'll never touch me now.

"I don't have to do this." It's almost like he's talking to himself.

"Do it for me," I whisper. "Let me. You were right before. We'll never see each other again after tonight. One way or another I'm going far away from here. Let me remember you like this. Not as the man who caught me. Let me remember you as the man…"

The words fall away as my throat closes. Tears sting my eyes. God, how embarrassing. I wanted to turn him on, and instead I'm crying.

"The man who let you go," he says roughly. "That's what you were going to say, isn't it?"

My nails dig into my palms. I can't even see him

through the tears. "No."

"Would you have given yourself to me so that I would let you go?" A stark pause. "Is that why you let me touch you."

"No!" But it's too late. I can tell he's already sure of it. I can feel his grief over it in the air. He swings away, his hand running over his face, frustration and guilt evident.

And that's when I know he isn't letting me go. It was a long shot, but how can he? He wouldn't be a Boy Scout anymore. Because that's what he is—I'm more sure now than ever. Even the orgasm he gave me was a twisted sort of gift. He can't change who he is any more than I can change who I am.

He's walking away now, and I'm sure he'll come back. He's pacing now, distressed.

I can't leave him that way. He shouldn't have to make that choice.

In one smooth move, I twist my wrist and turn my body the other way, freeing my arm from the chair in a matter of seconds. I use my free hand to tear the other piece of tape away, and then I'm grabbing the gun in a mad dash. I half expect West to get there before me, for him to be lunging toward the desk in a wild rush.

He isn't.

He's standing exactly where I last saw him, his expression more tired than angry.

And God, he isn't scared at all. Not even when I raise

the gun and point it at him. I don't know why I do it, exactly, except that it feels like what I'm supposed to do. I don't want to hurt him. I definitely don't want to shoot him, but as much as I care about him—and I do care, I can admit that now—I can't let myself be captured.

It's a question of survival, and I can see in his eyes he understands that.

His voice is steady. "Put that down, Bianca. It isn't safe."

A harsh laugh escapes me. "Isn't safe? You were pointing it at me earlier."

"I didn't point it at you, if you remember. And I have a lot more training with it than you do."

"That only means you can shoot me better. This is supposed to be comforting how?"

"I'm not going to shoot you."

"Yeah, because I have the gun." I have nothing if not bravado.

"I was never going to shoot you."

It's too much. "Then why did you have a gun with you?"

"I didn't know if you were going to come alone. Maybe you'd even send someone else. I had to be prepared for anything."

"Boy Scout." I mean it like an insult, but it just comes out sad.

"Bianca, listen to me. I asked around about you once I realized you were in trouble. I know something about the money—"

"Don't talk to me about the money."

He looks frustrated. "You don't understand. There aren't—"

"Just stop, okay? I'm not stealing from you. Not stealing from Ivan either."

As much as I hate the idea of stealing from him, of West knowing the truth about me, I can't forget that Jeb's life is on the line here. Maisie's too. Even mine. But I'd never be able to crack the safe and hold a gun on him at the same time. He'd turn the tables on me before then. The best I can hope for is to get away and figure something else to give the cartel.

His voice is low, and that damned earnestness is back on his handsome face. "You don't need to steal from anyone. I can help you."

"You don't know a damn thing," I whisper, but I'm already backing away, already working my way up the stairs. I don't want to hear anything else he has to say, fake promises that can never come true. There's no happy ending for someone like me. I'm a thief and a stripper. And once the mafia realizes I'm Jeb's daughter, I'm as good as dead.

When I get to the top of the stairs, I toss the gun aside and run for it. It's not my smoothest exit, but then everything about West twists me up.

I think he could have caught me. I know he could have.

But I make it out the front doors of the Grand, where the morning light has already split over downtown Tanglewod. Then I'm dashing down the street to where Maisie is waiting for me—waiting for me to hand over the money that would have kept us alive.

CHAPTER TWELVE

MAISIE KNOWS I don't have the money as soon as I show up. For one thing that much cash would be large and heavy, filling the expandable bag in my safecracking kit. And for another thing, I've been gone for hours. Breaking into a safe of that magnitude would take a while, but we're talking thirty minutes—not two hours.

It makes me wonder what she thought was happening all this time. Did she worry about me?

I know exactly what she was worried about.

"What am I going to tell the cartel?" she asks, already anxious. "You can go in again tomorrow night."

I shake my head, trying not to be disappointed. She didn't even ask if I'm okay when she must know *something* happened down in that basement. Maybe it had always been coming to this. Maybe this is what she wanted from me all along.

"They would be expecting me," I say, more tired than sad. "The code will be changed, the doors and locks reinforced. A trick like that only works once."

Actually it hadn't worked at all. West had seen me coming. "I have another idea."

Her expression is wary. "A way to get the money?"

"We go to Ivan." West wants me to trust him, but I'm too far gone for that. But I might be able to make a deal with Ivan—with the devil of Tanglewood. I'd probably have to sell my soul. That's all I deserve.

She gasps. "Bee, no."

"He'll be pissed when he finds out what we did." He might even kill us and save the Caivanos the trouble. "But we don't have any other options. At least Ivan knows I can earn money. I can work it off." Though I might have to do more than stripping to earn that kind of money in this lifetime. My stomach is a hard, twisted knot.

"I can't let you do that."

I'm actually touched that she's fighting this so hard. It's always been her and Jeb against the world. I was their daughter, but not a loved and cherished child. I was more like the getaway driver or the strategically placed distraction, someone useful to have around for a con—unless I wasn't.

The fact that she doesn't want to give me up to the cartel means more than it should. "It's the only way. I won't let Jeb die, and you too, when I could stop it."

"I'll find another way," she says, her voice rising. "I'll negotiate with them."

"They won't negotiate," I say softly. "Not after they've taken Jeb. It's gone too far for that."

"I'll talk to them," she says stubbornly.

Why won't she see? "At least let me go to Ivan first.

Then if I don't—" *If I don't make it out alive.* "If I don't come back, then you'll know it didn't work."

"You can't." Now she sounds almost petulant. It's a familiar tone but strange at a time like this. I know how much she loves Jeb. I've had reason to doubt her love for me, but never him.

"I don't understand," I mutter, almost to myself.

"She doesn't want you to understand." The voice comes from the end of the alley. A voice I recognize. A voice that very recently was murmuring dirty words against my clit.

West.

I whirl, blocking Maisie with my body. "Leave her alone."

"So protective." He's just a shadow, his body hidden by the building beside us. I can see he's holding something. My bag. I must have left it behind in my rush, which is foolish.

This entire thing is foolish.

We're deep in the alley, but the chain-link fence behind us doesn't provide any cover or protection. "I didn't take anything," I say, raising my chin. "And you had your fun. Let me go now."

He shakes his head. "I can't do that. Not when you're thinking of going with her."

The way he says *her* makes my gut clench. I know she hasn't been the best mother, but that's for me to decide. Not him. "How do you know who she is?"

"She's the one who sent you down to that basement.

And she left you there while I did whatever I wanted with you."

My insides turn cold. She did leave me there. She must have known it was taking longer than usual. Hell, she must have seen Blue when he left the Grand, proving I'd been caught.

She hadn't come in after me.

Logically I know there wouldn't have been any point to her getting caught too. The emotional side of me, the core of me is hurt that she let me suffer it alone. West didn't hurt me. No, he fed me and made me climax—but she couldn't know that about him.

I clench my hands into fists. "It's not your concern."

What I really mean is, *I'm not your concern.* Why should he care about me? No one else does.

He shakes his head, hearing exactly what I meant and denying it. "Someone has to look out for you," he says. "And it's not going to be her."

The words pierce me deeper this time, and I have to lash back. "She was doing what she had to do. You don't know what these people are capable of. They have my father."

"Are you sure about that?" The question is so soft I might not have heard it, but it echoes in my head as if he shouted it.

"Of course I'm sure."

Except now that he's asked the question, I don't know. Stealing fifty thousand dollars was a big fucking deal. It's not implausible he could be taken as collateral.

And more to the point, if Jeb hadn't been taken, why would Maisie lie?

As soon as I ask, I know the answer.

To get me to rob the Grand.

She and Jeb had proposed the idea when I first started working there, and I'd told her no. No fucking way. This was my chance to go straight, to earn an honest living, even if I did have to take my clothes off.

I turn to face her. Her expression tells me everything I need to know.

Glass cuts my insides. I need to hear the words. "Maisie?"

My voice is raw.

"Oh kid," she says softly. "You always cared too damn much. I told you that."

The air is too thick; I'm choking on it. Tears prick my eyes, and I can only stand there and stare at her. My mother. But not my mother. She may have given birth to me, but she has never loved me as a mother should. I could have forgiven her for leaving me down there with West, knowing what might have been happening. If she'd been desperate to save Jeb. But it turns out he wasn't captured.

The worst part is that it doesn't surprise me. This is who she is.

That doesn't keep it from hurting. The pain runs along deep ruts in my heart, places that have been trod over again and again. It's all I can do to stand upright in that alley, with trash and broken glass strewn around me like debris.

"Where is he?" I whisper.

She has the grace to blush. "At our motel room."

I picture the dried blood on his ring. Who cut themselves for that blood? "Does he know?"

"It was his idea." Her eyes shut against the pain—or what looks like pain. I can't tell anymore. I believed she was worried for Jeb, that she feared for his life, but that had been a lie. "The debt was real, but he was worried you wouldn't go through with it."

West moves in front of me, shielding me from her view. "Go," he says.

"What are you going to do with her?" I hear her ask. I can't even look anymore.

I never want to see her again.

"You lost the right to ask that question," he says. "Now get the fuck out of my sight before I call the cops."

I stare down at the ground, the glitter of wet rocks and the sheen of dewy puddles, as her footsteps fade away. Then there's only West and me in the alley, only the knowledge of what I did to him and what he did in return. And all my reasons, all my dreams turned to ash.

CHAPTER THIRTEEN

I WRAP MY fingers around the hot cup of…what is this? I breathe in the steam. Tea.

West pushed it into my hand a few minutes after sitting me down on his couch. He wrapped a thick afghan throw over my shoulders. Now he's in the kitchen, speaking in low tones to someone on the phone. Probably Blue. He'll have to explain why I'm not in police custody—or worse.

It doesn't seem to matter anymore, what happens to me. Lock me up. Throw away the key. It's not like I had some great future ahead of me. It's not like I have anyone who'll care when I'm gone.

West enters the large open living space, tossing his phone onto a side table. His apartment is a huge loft in the part of Tanglewood undergoing a resurgence. Old buildings are being remodeled and rented out. This place has exposed brick and stainless steel. It wouldn't have come cheap.

If I had pictured him anywhere, it would have been in a simple, bare apartment one step up from my own. And I would have been wrong. The walls could use some artwork, but the place is fully furnished in the kind of restrained, comfortable style that speaks of money.

My faded bag looks ridiculous leaning against the side of the plush, luxurious sofa.

He looks down at my tea, his expression disapproving. "Drink."

I consider making a dirty joke about that or maybe just flat out refusing. Except what would be the point? He proved in that basement that he could master me if he chooses. And after what happened in that alley... *Don't think about that.*

After what happened in that alley, I don't really have any fight left in me.

I take a sip. The hot liquid burns its way down, but it doesn't touch the chill inside me.

West's frown deepens. He sits across from me on the rustic wood coffee table. I barely feel the cup leave me fingers as he sets it aside.

"Bianca. Talk to me."

I tilt my head. "About what?"

He gives me a low laugh, almost like he's laughing at himself. "About what happened in that alley. About what I did to you in that basement. Hell, you can talk to me about the weather if you want to. I just need to hear your voice. I need to know you're okay."

"I'm not okay."

He swears under his breath. "Shit. After what your parents did, of course you're not."

"How do you know she's my parent?"

He gives me a self-deprecating look. "I'm not blind.

As much as I've tried to be since I started working at the Grand. It's hard to miss the resemblance."

"Yeah." My voice sounds hollow. "I've always looked like her."

I've always *been* like her, using my body and my smile to get what doesn't belong to me. I tried to change. I tried to go straight, but look where that got me.

He swears again. "I should have had her arrested."

I feel strangely numb, as if I'm only watching things happen. "Why didn't you?"

"It would have been complicated to explain your involvement. And we would have had to go down to the police station tonight."

I pull the afghan tighter around my shoulders, grateful I'm at his loft instead of a cold police station. "What are you going to do with me?"

"Right now? I'm going to put you to bed. You're falling asleep just sitting there."

"You were never going to turn me in, were you?" I say suddenly, already knowing it's true.

He shakes his head slowly. "We got word that someone was offering cash for the security code. Blue had the idea to give it to them, to set the ambush and catch them in the act."

And then I really would have been in a jail cell tonight. "You didn't let him. Why?"

Because he wanted to fuck me? He didn't even do that. Because he wanted to *taste* me? There were easier ways to accomplish that.

Hope beats in my breast that maybe it's something more. Maybe it's because he cares about me. I've spent my whole life stealing or being stolen from, being a thief or being a mark. I could never trust him. Never trust anyone.

"You need rest," he says gently. "We can talk in the morning."

And just like that the hope quiets.

Even if he did care about me before, how could he now? And even if he did still care, how could he ever trust me? I've ruined the only good thing I ever had, before I even knew I had it.

And I realize it isn't about whether I can trust in him. I already know he's good. My knight in shining armor. The question is whether I'm worthy of him, whether I deserve this—and I know the answer to that too. I've been nothing but a thief and a liar my whole life, from the moment I came out of the womb. Worthless.

CHAPTER FOURTEEN

I WAKE TO a soft sound in the pitch-black. It takes me a minute to realize where I am. Not on my narrow bed with my thin, old sheets—but in West's bed, a wide, plush mattress topped with butter-soft sheets. It smells faintly of him, spice and skin. I wish he were here with me, but I know without reaching for the other side of the bed that he's not.

The soft sound draws my attention to the window, where rain has begun to fall. It's still too warm to snow, but the glass, when I press my palm against it, feels like ice.

There's no alarm clock cutting through the dark. I gave up carrying my phone around when I could no longer afford prepaid minutes. I don't know what time it is. The darkness and the rain make it feel like we're locked in an eternal night, even though it must be morning soon.

Most of the loft is a wide-open space. Only a few rooms are walled off—this bedroom, the bathroom, and the kitchen. I find West on the same couch that he comforted me on, the afghan have covering his jean-clad legs, his chest bare.

One arm is flung above his head, the other dropped over the side to the floor.

He looks comfortable and secure, the opposite of how I feel in these clothes I used to betray him. They're comfortable enough for sleeping, but they're a reminder of how I broke us apart.

His tattoos are barely visible in the darkness, only shadows whispering over his skin. I'd seen hints of them before, peeking out from his T-shirts, and I can't see much more now. I trace one dark line down his bicep, but he doesn't stir.

What would he do if he woke up? Would he send me back to bed? Or maybe I would have gotten enough rest for his conscious. He could send me away then.

I have no illusions that we're going to last. That anything could happen between us now.

There's an intimacy between us after what happened last night. After he put his mouth on me and protected me. That intimacy will fade under the cold glare of a winter morning, but it's still here.

And I want to return the favor.

I let my finger keep going, over the ridges of his abs, down to the bulge in his jeans. Morning wood. He didn't let me touch him last night. That damned sense of honor strikes again. It can't stop me now. I'm not tied up, and more importantly, I've already proven I don't deserve any honorable treatment.

His cock swells beneath the zipper as I stroke him, but his arms and face don't move. He's feeling the pleasure, but he isn't waking up. I prefer it that way, because he can't judge me while he's sleeping. He can only feel what I give him.

The denim is stretched taut now, so tight it's hard to pull the zipper down without hurting him. His cock springs free, heavy and hard in my hands, warming me.

This answers the boxers-or-briefs question. Neither.

My thumb brushes over the tip, finding a well of salty liquid. I smooth the precum over the head of his cock, and his hips push up in unconscious response.

I kneel beside the couch, fisting him.

I don't imagine that I have some special talent in this area. I'm only eighteen, which doesn't leave a lot of room for experience, despite the fact that I started early—not every con goes smoothly, after all. Or someone needs a little extra incentive to provide a security code or guard schedule. My innocence was bartered early and often. Because we had to. Necessity. The same excuses Maisie had last night, but I'm done believing her. Even if it means I have to be alone.

I'm not alone now. For now I have West. I have his harsh breathing and his tense body. I have his cock that feels like molten steel against my palm.

Leaning forward, I taste him—a sharp, salty flavor that I know I'll never forget.

A low groan comes from his chest, more of a rumble than a moan, but he still doesn't stir. I might be in his dreams right now, a girlfriend from his past or some fantasy creation. Or I might be any one of the girls he's brought home for the night. There must have been many.

It's not really me he's feeling, but I'm feeling him. The silky softness at the crown of his cock, the velvet thin skin that covers his shaft. The tight black hair that brushes against my hand every time my fist presses down.

His rough sounds fill the air around me, a symphony of sex and man.

He's close to coming. I can tell by the way his thighs are trembling, by the hard bunch of his abs. His whole body is canted on the edge of climax.

That's when I realize his arms are no longer flung carelessly over his head or over the side of the couch. They're held tight by his body, hands curled into fists. *He's holding himself back.*

He's awake.

I pause, my lips sliding over the ridge of him as I look up. His eyes are still closed, his face taut—he looks like he's in pain. When I stop moving, his eyes fly open. They're black in the darkness, but I can read the hunger in them. The need.

"Bianca," he says hoarsely.

There's desperation in that word. Affection too.

No surprise. He knew it was me all along. He might have been awake the whole time. When will I learn that I can't catch him off guard? I've conned a hundred men out of their money, in lots of different ways. I always knew that one would eventually catch me, hurt me, break me.

West has done those things, but not like I thought it would be. He doesn't hurt me.

No, he's infinitely gentle as he runs the side of his finger along my temple and trails a lock of my hair. He's shaking with need, but he doesn't force my head or thrust up into me. He pushes the strands between his thumb and forefinger. "So fucking soft," he mutters.

I lean forward to finish what I started, but he stops me. "What's wrong?"

He swallows audibly. "I need to come, baby. I need you so bad."

But when I press forward again, his hands hold me back.

"Not like that," he murmurs.

Then I'm twisting, falling, lying flat on my back where he used to be, his leftover heat rising up to meet me while his body bears me down.

CHAPTER FIFTEEN

I EXPECT HIM to push inside of me, to start fucking me and take what he deserves. I don't have much of anything to offer him. Only my body.

He helps himself to my body but not how I expect. Instead he kisses his way over my breasts and down my stomach. They're mere brushes of his lips that tease more than they pleasure. Then he bends his head between my legs, and I can't help but spread them wider. I don't deserve what he's going to do to me, but I crave it.

"You don't..." I manage to gasp out. "You don't have to."

He groans, dark eyes meeting mine. His voice is pure gravel. "You think I'm doing this just for you? You think I haven't fucking dreamed about this every night since I first saw you dance?"

He seems to be waiting for answer. "I...don't know?"

"I've been dreaming of how you'll taste. And after having you, I'm fucking addicted. Even down in that basement, I couldn't wait to have you again. Somewhere warm and soft, where I know you'll be comfortable for a long, long time."

"Oh." I feel faint, just thinking about how long he

might be planning on licking me. What happened in that basement is already the longest I've ever imagined a man's mouth on me—and it drove me insane with pleasure. What could he do to me with all the time in the world?

He doesn't seem to want to discuss it anymore.

No, he clearly intends to show me.

He doesn't start off soft like he did before. Not testing or tasting. He plunges his tongue into my slit as fiercely as I thought he'd do with his cock—as if he's dying to feel my heat, my softness. He gathers up all my juices on his tongue, and then he forces me to make more.

I reach back and hold on to the sofa as if it can anchor me, but the force of his will is too strong. One lick on my clit, then two. When he presses his lips around my clit and sucks, I push off the couch and climax in long, draining pulses that leave me sated.

He's not done with me.

His mouth never leaves my flesh. He drinks my orgasm down, then immediately starts pushing me toward another one.

"No," I gasp. "Too much." I'm too sensitive, feeling too much pleasure. Who would have known it could feel like pain? I've never had anyone give me enough to find out.

Large hands press my legs down, and he feasts on me.

I'm trembling and crying out by the time I come again, bucking against him, fucking his mouth.

My body collapses on the couch, still shaking from the aftershocks. And he doesn't let up. I look down and see the wicked glint in his eyes. He loves tasting me, loves making me come so hard my muscles turn to jelly. Over and over again. This is why I needed to be somewhere warm—because I'm shivering when I'm not in the middle of climax. This is why I needed to be somewhere soft. I sink into the cushions and let them carry me away, pleasure like waves lapping at my skin.

I can't keep track of how many times he makes me come. At some point I think they aren't even separate times, but one long stretch of bliss. I feel incandescent, glowing from the inside, the heat from my climaxes visible through my skin.

His hands press down on the inside of my thighs, tighter as he fights for control, and I know he'll leave bruises. He's hurting me, and he's hurting himself. It's part of the game he plays with us, taking us both higher.

Just when I think I can't take any more—that he can't take any more—he kneels between my legs.

With one hand he notches his cock against my slick entrance. With his other hand, he grabs my hip, steadying me. Only then do I realize my hips are moving on their own, fucking the air—I'm that far gone to this, to sex. To him.

He presses inside me. When he's all the way inside, he groans. It sounds like agony. "No condom."

"Don't stop." I'm not even sure I've formed the words correctly. I may have just made an urgent sound, a desperate sound, but he seems to understand.

His eyes are almost pitch-black with need. "Are you sure?"

I squeeze him with my inner muscles, and that's all the answer he needs. He starts fucking me hard, rocking the whole couch with each thrust. The force of his thrusts push me up the sofa until I'm tipping over the side. I let my head and shoulders hang over the edge, reveling in the pure savagery.

Then I feel his hard chest meet my breasts. His hand cups the back of my head, and he's holding me up, holding me to him while he kisses me. It's a tender kiss, a sharp contrast to the way his body slams into mine.

He fucks me until I sob his name and come around him. I milk his orgasms right out of him because he follows right behind, his rough groan like music—a haunting tune I know I'll think of later, when he's gone.

When he pulls out, he looks down, and I do too. My sex is flushed pink and swollen with the pounding he's given me. His cock is dark, almost purple at the tip, and shiny from his come.

His come. He came inside me. *No condom.*

His gaze acknowledges the loss, but he doesn't look worried. He looks satisfied, almost smug. "You're mine now."

Chapter Sixteen

H E LETS ME wash up, a short reprieve. I clean myself with water and soap, but they do nothing to diminish the feel of him coming inside me, the insistent jet of come that marks me as his. It was a primitive feeling—skin to skin, the hot wash of come.

I feel claimed even though I don't believe in things like that.

I search through his drawers and find a large pair of cotton workout shorts and a white T-shirt that hangs off one shoulder. They're too big for me, but I don't mind. They're like armor, and I need all the protection I can get. I'm too exposed right now, too vulnerable in every way that matters—at least I can pretend that my body is still my own.

When I come back into the living space, he's on the phone in the kitchen.

He paces, vibrating with tension. "We need to find him before he—"

There's a pause.

"I can't take that risk," West says, practically growling. "I don't even want to leave her alone until they're gone."

Another pause.

Then a sigh. "Yeah, I got it. Thank you. I mean it."

It must be Blue on the other end of the line. I can tell by the familiar way West speaks, full of trust and friendship. I linger in the living room, knowing I shouldn't be listening. It's like the laughter I heard at the baby shower—alluring but not for me.

He hangs up and notices me. His expression flashes blank fast enough that I know exactly who he was talking about with Blue. *Me.*

"You're looking for Jeb?" I ask.

He doesn't flinch, but his expression is wary. He comes closer. "We need to make sure they're not going to target the Grand anymore."

"It's okay." It's only natural they would be looking for Jeb. I'm surprised he let Maisie leave at all. Maybe some old-world chivalry thing. But Maisie is just as guilty as Jeb—and I'm as guilty as them both. "I understand."

"You do?"

"You have to do your job and protect the Grand." And I'm not going to fight him or evade him. Not anymore. He can fuck me until he's ready to turn me over to Ivan. Or maybe he'll let me go. I don't even care anymore. They're both the same. They both mean losing him.

"That's right." His voice is cautious.

"And you want to make sure we leave the city," I continue, my voice cracking. "That's only fair, considering what we tried to do."

His expression darkens. "You're not leaving, Bianca. Not when I just got you here."

I bite my lip. "I don't understand. Why would you want to keep me after what I did?"

The obvious answer is my body, but I don't fool myself. There's an entire club full of beautiful girls at the Grand—girls who never tried to steal. He's sexy and kind. He would have no trouble finding a girl to sleep with him. There's no reason why he should want me.

Though, he doesn't look like he wants me. Not at the moment. He looks angry.

"God, Bianca. You really can't believe anyone wants to help you? To be with you?"

I flinch because he's right.

He pulls me to the sofa. "Baby, you're an incredible woman. Strong. Smart. Obviously gorgeous. Any man would trip over his dick trying to be with you." He makes a face. "I should have said that better."

I smile, feeling shy. "I think you said it pretty great."

He sighs. "I hate that you doubt yourself, that you won't let yourself trust me."

A knot tightens my throat. "I do trust you."

As much as I trust anyone, which admittedly isn't much.

His eyes study mine. "When I first met you, I wanted to be with you. And the way you looked at me, it seemed like you wanted me too."

"I did." At his wry expression, I laugh a little. How

can he make me laugh, even now? "I *do* want you."

"But every time I got close, you backed away. At first I was going to respect that. No matter that you looked at me like you wanted to touch me, no matter that I was dying to taste you."

My eyebrows go up. "I was a little surprised that you…you know. Did that. While I was tied up."

He gets a strange expression, and I have the feeling that if I touched his cheeks they would be warm. He's blushing. "Then I saw you struggling and refusing help from anyone—not from me or the other girls. You were getting thinner, and I could see the fear in your eyes. Then you went and tried to steal from the Grand—"

"I'm so sorry," I whisper.

"I'm not angry, baby. I'm just explaining why I couldn't hold back any more. I couldn't watch you destroy yourself. I came to care about you, despite you pushing me away, despite my best efforts not to care, and I couldn't let anyone hurt you—not even yourself."

I shiver. "And not my parents."

"Definitely not them." His expression turns cold, and I realize this is the face of the soldier, the man who fought multiple tours overseas. This is what his enemies saw. "They should have protected you."

"I'm not going to defend them. I spent too long giving them excuses."

"You don't ever need to see them again." The way he says it, I can almost believe it's true.

I look down at my loose T-shirt and shorts rolled up

at the waistband. I feel even more helpless without my clothes. That's just an illusion, though. I was already as helpless as possible, whether I'm wearing flip-flops or stilettos or nothing at all. "What about me?"

He looks down, seeming almost vulnerable. "I hope you'll stay with me." He pauses. "At least until the New Year. We don't have to decide anything right away, and you'll be safe here. I'll have Blue send someone to bring your clothes."

It can't be that simple. "What about Ivan?"

"What about him?"

"Umm, I broke into his club."

"Only because we let you." West smiles a little at my glare. Then he sobers. "Ivan doesn't have to know."

"He might find out. You'd lose your job." I don't add that he would more likely lose his life.

A fierce light enters his eyes. "I'll protect you from anyone, Bianca. And I'll just need to keep saying it until you believe me. If Ivan came after you, I'd keep you safe. If anyone even thinks about touching you, I'd make them wish they were never born."

There he is again, the warrior. It makes me shiver. "Okay," I whisper.

"Good." He smiles, looking almost normal. Like a hot guy you'd meet at a coffee shop—not terrifying and intense. Not like he's going to battle the world just to keep me alive. "Now come have breakfast. Do you want omelets or pancakes? Wait, what am I saying? I'll make both."

Chapter Seventeen

B REAKFAST IS JUST the beginning, and I spend the rest of the day cocooned in a warmth I've only dreamed about. I find a box of microwave popcorn in the pantry, and West pulls out a needle and thread from an impressive first-aid kit. We create edible garland that we string up around his loft, adding a bit of festive charm to the stark space.

His expression is so focused as he pushes the needle through the puffy kernels, as if he's on the battlefield, as if it's a question of life or death. So I can't help but toss a kernel at him, which bounces off his broad and impressively solid chest.

He looks up, first in surprise, then in mischievous delight—he retaliates with a hail of popcorn fire.

Then the bowl is empty, and I'm flat on the rug, laughing, popcorn in my hair. I'm a disaster, but he looks down at me like I'm the most beautiful thing he's ever seen.

It's strange and rare, and I would give anything to stay like this forever.

Even now, in pure bliss, there's a frantic edge, an undertone of dread, because it will never be enough.

His phone chimes, and I feel him tense above me. He backs off me, and I immediately miss the safety of his arms, the surety of his weight. His body moves stiffly as he crosses the room to check the text message, as if whatever's happening pains him. Or worries him.

What could worry a man as strong and sure as this one?

"What's wrong?" I ask softly.

He looks at me, and a shadow crosses his face. I know he feels the loss of intimacy, of warmth as much as I do. "We think your parents skipped town."

"Oh." The thought makes my stomach clench, even though I don't want to see them again. Abandonment never really gets easier. It's just less of a surprise.

He pauses, his expression guarded. "We found the motel room they'd been renting. It had some schematics of the Grand and other items that identify them."

Guilt and shame war within me. I'm embarrassed that I ever tried to rob the club. I'm glad we failed. The Grand was never really at risk anyway. We only got that far inside because West had been setting a trap.

I fold my arms across myself. "Maybe you could just… let them go. They didn't take anything."

His expression is dark. "That's not the problem."

Realization dawns. "The money. Fifty thousand dollars. That's what they told me Jeb owed the Caivano family. Maisie said…she said they were holding him hostage until they got their money."

"The Caivano family doesn't take hostages."

"No," I agree quietly. If I had been thinking straight I might have realized that. The Caivano family isn't known for their patience. Or their mercy. They would have killed Jeb if they could have gotten their hands on him. "Maisie showed me his ring as proof that he was taken. I was so worried."

My voice cracks on the last word. It makes my stomach turn over to think about them planning to con me—about him giving her his ring just to make sure I went through with the job. I'm a fool for ever worrying about him.

For ever loving him, even if he is my father.

Anger flashes through West's eyes. "With them gone…"

With them gone, the Caivanos will be out for blood. And I'm the only one left. "So I'm in trouble," I say, trying to sound light.

I want him to tell me I'm wrong. I want him to tell me I'm safe.

"Your apartment was searched," he says instead.

My stomach turns over as I imagine my crappy apartment in tatters. There wasn't much there—my clothes and some old pictures. Piles of yarn that I mostly unravel from antique clothing I find at garage sales.

My throat feels tight. "I guess it was always going to end like this."

West's expression is fierce. "No one will touch you."

I shake my head while he's speaking, because he can't protect me forever. "Don't worry about me." My voice rings false. "I've looked after myself this long."

"You'll stay here," he says. "We're looking for your parents, and Blue has contacts with the Caivano family to see if we can work something out. I'm looking after you now."

Even the conviction in his words can't comfort me now.

Panic has been steadily building. I feel violated. I feel terrified.

I want more popcorn and more wrestling. I want more of that foreign, bursting feeling inside my chest. Stolen moments before I have to return the wreckage of my own life. So I nod in silence.

His arm tightens around me. He says nothing either.

There are no promises made, no lies I can pretend to believe. As soon as this interlude is over, I'll be back on the street—penniless and, after my apartment was sacked, homeless. The people looking for me will find me then.

CHAPTER EIGHTEEN

FOR THAT DAY and the next we exist in a bubble full of great food and great sex. By tacit agreement we both avoid talking about my parents or Ivan or anything too sharp.

When I sit down for dinner a few days later, I know the bubble has burst.

The food looks amazing—steaks and a crisp, green asparagus. There's a small chocolate cake waiting to be cut into. A hidden stereo system streams the "Christmas Canon." It's almost a celebration, but I'm not fooled. There's something simmering beneath the surface.

It feels more like a last meal.

"What's wrong?" I ask West's back. He hasn't turned from the salad he's tossing even though I know he senses me here. He always seems to know where I am.

When he turns, I see the truth in his expression. It's time for me to leave. "I have to go out," he says instead. And I'm surprised but not relieved—I feel the end drawing near.

"Did something happen?" What I mean is, *Did you find Jeb and Maisie?*

It's kind of sick that I hope they won't be found. If

they are found by the Caivano family, they'll be killed. But if they aren't found, I'll have to answer for their debt.

West looks grim. "I won't know until I see for myself."

"Can I come with you?" I'm afraid at what we might find at this mystery destination, but this is my mess. My problem. I got him into this, it's only fair I be there with him.

He shakes his head. "It's too dangerous. I'd rather you stay here."

Dangerous. It is dangerous for me here, but not for the reasons he thinks. It's dangerous to feel acceptance, to feel love. It's dangerous for someone like me to hope. "You'd be with me."

"I don't know what I'll find there. Here there's a security system and a dead bolt. And a pistol in that drawer." He nods to the corner. "This is the safest place you can be."

I can't help the relief I feel. I don't want to see Jeb or Maisie if they're hurt. And I definitely don't want to see them if they're alive. There's a part of me that doesn't even trust myself. That if I see them, I'll fall prey to whatever con they try to run, to whatever lies they tell. The desire to have parents who care runs deep, an ache that will never really go away.

It's like a stay of execution. I'll have to leave eventually, but not now. Not yet.

"You'll be careful," I implore softly. If it could be

dangerous for me, it could be dangerous for him. I know how skilled he is, but Jeb has gotten himself in deep. I've gotten in deep too.

He nods, looking more determined than worried, my knight in shining armor.

And I'll be alone in the castle tower.

"After dinner?" I ask, my voice small.

He seems relieved too, that I didn't put up a fight. He must not realize how desperately I want to stay here, how much I've come to love this place—and him. He gives me a kiss on the forehead before sitting beside me. "After dinner."

I want to believe I have a future with West, that he'll be safe, that I will too. But the past has its hooks in me too deep. I'm no princess.

I don't deserve a fairy-tale ending.

CHAPTER NINETEEN

THERE'S NOT MUCH to do in West's apartment—except snoop. I'm curious about him, but it turns out I don't want to find out anything he doesn't want me to know. He trusted me, even when I didn't deserve it. I'll make sure he can trust me now.

I spot my faded leather bag tucked into a corner by the sofa. For a second, I wonder if that could be what the men are after. But there's nothing but old tools that any lock pick would have.

And yarn.

I pull out the dark red yarn, already half-formed into a hat. Actually, it would make a lovely Christmas gift for West—and I wonder if I'd been subconsciously making it for him all along. The rich color would look beautiful against his dark skin.

Then I think about the soft strands wrapped *around* him, like tied around his wrists, and I realize I can make something else with this yarn. It only takes a few minutes to undo the work I've done so far, and then I start on something better, something darker—a thick braided rope.

When it's finished it will still be soft, but it will also

be strong.

I'm deep in my work, fingers working nimbly when I hear the knock. I freeze.

Carefully, as if it might break, I set the needles and yarn down on a table. My heart pounds when I spot Jeb through the peephole. I don't open the door.

He knows I'm there anyway. "Bee? Open up, sweetheart."

I dial West on the mobile phone he gave me, but there's no answer. I text him, *Jeb is here.*

I'm protected against someone storming the castle walls. What West didn't count on is that Jeb wouldn't try to hide. What West didn't count on is that my own heart would want to betray him, a little girl who's overjoyed that her daddy didn't leave her after all.

He'll have a good reason for what happened, my heart says. He'll fix everything.

My heart lies.

I turn away from the door, turn away from him, but I'm still just two feet away. Close enough to hear what he has to say. I can't deny that I'm curious. He's my father. Shouldn't he love me? Shouldn't he care? Except he doesn't, not if he put my life at risk.

"I know what happened at the club," he continues, speaking a little louder than normal to be heard through the door. It makes me wonder if West's neighbors can hear him, but I doubt it. These old buildings were built to withstand anything. "I'll get you out of there."

The way he says it, it's as if he's trying to rescue me.

Instead it sounds like a threat.

A laugh escapes me that sounds more like a sob. I don't think he could hear that through the door, but it doesn't really matter. He'd rather hear himself talk than me anyway.

"That guy's been keeping you in here for two days. We've been waiting for the chance to get you out. Open the door, Bee. Whatever he's told you, whatever he's done to you, it doesn't matter now."

That's where he's wrong. West told me I was worth something—worth loving, worth risking everything for. And he backed it up with his actions. He's been nothing but kind to me. That matters. It means the world to me.

"Bee." A pause, and I can picture the crestfallen look on his face. So practiced. "We can be a family again."

I should have stayed silent. I planned to, when I saw him at the door. It's too much though. I whirl and face the door, imagining it's him. The wood might as well be nothing, because I can see him—in that casual but concerned slouch he's affected. The perfect con, even for his daughter.

"We were never a family," I say to the door.

"Open up, Bee," he says, and there's a tremor in his voice this time. I could almost believe he's emotional over me, except I know better. It took me eighteen years to see my father for what he is. So if he's not having a heart-wrenching moment with his only child, what made his voice waver?

And then I have my answer. I hear scuffling from the

other side. I look through the peephole in time to see Jeb being grabbed by large hands.

"You had your chance to convince her," says a man big enough to block out the screen. He's up close—and he's holding a gun to Jeb's head. They're both distorted, the middle made large, as if I'm in a dream. A nightmare. "Come out, come out, little girl. Your daddy wants to see you."

There's a metallic taste in my mouth, and I realize I've bit my tongue.

I've never seen the man before in my life, but it's clear from the confident way he handles the gun, and the bulk of his body, that he means business. God, he brought these people here. He brought them here to take me as payment for his debt. I'm sick with it. I'm furious.

And I can't let Jeb die right in front of me.

Even though he brought this danger to my door. Even though he risks my life at every turn. I see my father for what he is now, but I still can't let him die. Even if it makes me soft and weak and *a mark*— everything I've been taught to look down upon—this is who I am. Someone who will disarm the alarm and open the locks, trading my own life for his.

"Don't hurt him," I say softly, opening the door.

This is the opposite of *trading up*, giving myself in exchange for him. The opposite of what my mother would do. And that's how I know it's right.

The guy has a scar down the side of his face. It makes his smile look like a snarl. "Now why would I do that, little girl? I've got a bigger prize now."

He pushes Jeb down, and he stumbles, looking older than I've ever seen him. A large hand grabs my arm, and he whirls me around.

West is standing at the edge of the hallway. Blue is behind him, along with a couple of other men from the security team. And farther back is Maisie, her eye blackened and her dress torn.

"Jeb," she cries. Even now she only has eyes for him as he struggles to stand. The fact that there's a gun to my temple doesn't even seem to register.

It does to West though. He sends a look to the man holding me that feels like pure ice.

This is the warrior who fought overseas. *This is the killer.*

I can't let him get hurt for me. I *won't* let him get hurt.

He would have charged us, would have been my knight in shining armor—and earned a bullet in the heart. I would have traded my life for my father's and ended up dead.

We would have written our own tragedies.

I used to think I didn't deserve a fairy-tale ending, but in this moment I realize they aren't only for the princess. It doesn't matter who our parents are, doesn't matter whether we dance at a ball or strip onstage. All that matters is that we have the courage to reach for it.

And by God, I will not let West die in this hallway. I will not let them win. That's the last coherent thought I have before I jam my elbow into the large stomach behind me. It's mostly muscle and doesn't get far, but it does startle the guy holding me enough to loosen his hold.

I turn in his grasp and knee his balls—that's one benefit of working in a strip joint for so long. I know how to handle a man who's getting handsy, even one who's also holding a gun. He goes down, staggering into the wall.

The guy next to him tries to grab me, but he only gets one step closer before red blooms on his shirt and he staggers back. I curl myself into the door frame as shots boom through the corridor.

The silence rings so loud, it takes me a second to realize the shooting is over. All I can hear now is the groaning of men in pain—the ones that aren't ominously still and silent.

Jeb is holding his arm and whimpering. There was a time I would have run to him.

Now I look away. He's a stranger to me, worse than that.

A large body blocks my view, and I'm disappointed to find that it's Blue. He guides me inside, but I fight him. I have to see West.

"He needs to do this," Blue says solemnly. "You shouldn't watch."

Chapter Twenty

"**T**HREE...TWO...ONE...."

I blink groggily at the large flat-screen TV while the distant sound of fireworks booms through the ground. West looks down at me with a soft, indulgent smile. "Happy New Year."

My sleep schedule was messed up after working at the Grand every night and then abruptly stopping. Instead of staying up late, I've taken to falling asleep early. "I'm sorry," I murmur. "I wanted to stay up with you."

West kisses my nose. "You need rest."

It's been a couple of days since a man was killed outside the door of this loft. Self-defense, everyone assured the cops who came to take the body away. They kept the story short and sweet.

West made sure that Jeb left town—possibly with his fists—and Maisie went with him, of course. Empty handed. This is one time they didn't *trade up*.

I already know they'll never come back.

I would never help them again, and there's nothing worthwhile about a daughter you can't con.

The first night, West took me into the shower with

him, carefully washing me, checking my skin for any marks or bruises. He touched me so tenderly, as if I was made of glass. And maybe I was. It felt like I might shatter.

Although he was hard and slick, he didn't have sex with me. Even when I touched him, he pushed my hand aside. He held me all night, his body tense and protective around mine.

Maybe we both needed a little time to recover, to heal.

It's a new year now. A new beginning. And though I'm sleepy, I drape my leg over his and straddle him. His eyes immediately turn black. He's been hard every time we've touched.

His face is drawn with intense arousal—but there's worry too.

"I need this more," I whisper.

He swallows audibly, and I know he's fighting himself. A week ago he tied my wrists to a chair and pressed his lips between my legs. He treated me like a woman, and that's what I need from him now.

I take his wrists in my hands and press them down on the cushions. Then I meet his gaze, a challenge arcing from me to him. He could overpower me in a second. If I hold him captive, it's only because he wants me to.

Acceptance curves his lips.

Then I'm working at the placket of his jeans, opening the zipper and pulling him out. He's already hard beyond anything I'd seen before. His cock stands straight up, straining for me. A bead of liquid shines at the tip. I lick it off.

He groans. "Baby."

"I need you," I murmur, lips moving against the soft crown. Then I take him deep, gratified by his pained groan. His legs shake beneath my palms. I don't let up. The more he shudders, the more I suck. Out of the corner of my eyes, I see his hands tighten into fists against the cushion—but he doesn't lift them. He doesn't push my head down, and I appreciate that. But I also miss his touch, the way he would stroke my hair or caress me. I miss his tenderness. I even miss his control.

I pull back with a *pop* sound, and he grunts.

His voice is like gravel. "You're killing me."

That makes me grin. "Just returning the favor."

He's up in a flash, slipping a hand under my arms and lifting me into the air. I'm over his shoulder before I can blink, and I writhe, trying to break free, laughing. "Let me down."

He slaps my ass. "I'm not letting you go, Bianca. You have a bad habit of running."

Guilty as charged. I remember him pressing me against the brick wall in the alley. I remember his hands holding down my thighs as he brought me to ecstasy in the basement of the Grand. It feels like a lifetime ago—a lifetime without love, without hope. A whole lifetime without family. I couldn't believe that he could really want me. I couldn't believe that he would really stay.

He didn't give up on me. And I have a lifetime to

thank him.

He tosses me on his bed, and I bounce. He's on me in a second, his legs between mine. His broad shoulders block the light, and I look up at him in shadow—this powerful, beautiful man.

Trade up. I traded in everything, everything that I used to be, everything that I never wanted to be, for the most honorable man I've ever met. Ironic that the first time I ever follow my mother's advice is when she's left for good.

West may be physically stronger than me, but he'd never force me. He'd never hurt me.

Which is why he doesn't fight when I turn the tables.

It's the quick work of my leg hooked around his, taking him by surprise—and then he's on his back on the bed. What can I say? My parents knew some unsavory people. I learned how to protect myself.

West huffs a laugh, sounding reluctantly impressed. "So that's how it's gonna be."

"That's exactly how it's gonna be." With a small flourish I pull out the package I'd hidden under the bed. It's only wrapped in newspaper since I hadn't had the chance to buy wrapping paper. I hold it out for him, feeling unaccountably shy.

His expression turns bemused as he accepts the small, padded square. Then he rips open the paper. First there's tenderness as he fingers the soft, red rope. Then a dark awareness lights his eyes. "Is this for…?"

"Yes," I say, taking the rope from his hands. And

then I do more than tell him—I show him, binding his wrists with the stretchy, knitted rope. The red is vibrant against his dark brown skin, a vivid contrast of con-strained power. He's a contradiction—the Boy Scout and the warrior, the gentle lover and the fierce man who tied me to a chair.

He caught me in the basement of the Grand, and I've caught him right back.

The con of a lifetime.

THANK YOU

Thank you for reading Caught for Christmas. I hope you loved West and Bianca's story!

The next book in the Stripped series is Hold You Against Me, which includes the series prequel novella Tough Love. You can click through and read Giovanni and Clara's story now...

> "Hold You Against Me quite literally grabs a hold and refuses to let go until the end. Truly one of the first Mafia books I've read that sucked me in with a completely original and brilliant storyline that had me guessing the entire time!"
>
> ~ #1 NYT Bestselling Author Rachel Van Dyken

Once upon a time the daughter of a mafia king fell in love with a foot soldier.

This fairy tale didn't have a happy ending.

My sister and I barely managed to escape alive, and we've lived in relative hiding ever since. I'm safe now, but I can never forget the boy who gave his life to save mine.

Except there's a chance that he's still alive. And he's fighting a war.

Even knowing the risks, I have to find him. I have to

find some way to protect him, the way he protected me. But he isn't the boy I left behind. He's a violent man. A criminal. And he's been waiting for me—the final pawn in a dark game of survival and love.

Be sure you sign up for my newsletter so you can find out when I have new releases and sales!

You can also join my Facebook group, Skye Warren's Dark Room, to discuss Caught for Christmas, the Stripped series, and my other books.

I appreciate your help in spreading the word, including telling a friend. Reviews help readers find books! Please leave a review on your favorite book site.

Turn the page to read a short excerpt from Hold You Against Me...

EXCERPT FROM
HOLD YOU AGAINST ME

SOMETHING MOVES ME gently, constant and rhythmic like waves. I'm warm. There's something soft curling around my arms, wrapped inside my fists. Padding beneath my cheek that smells like home.

An unnatural darkness weighs down on me, keeping me from waking up—a demon's whisper in my ear. *You're warm, you're safe. Sleep.*

But something is wrong.

I remember falling asleep, so suddenly, remember drinking water that I hadn't filled. And I remember the phone call from Amy telling me that Giovanni's alive. Impossible.

Awareness pricks my skin like a cold breeze. Wherever I am, I'm not alone.

I blink rapidly, forcing my eyes open. They adjust to the darkness quickly, taking in the tinted windows on either side and the wide leather bench curving beneath me. I'm in a car. A limo, to be exact. And it's moving.

On the opposite side of the long space, a large body reclines. I can see the wide stance of his legs, the pale white of his shirt. A suit jacket tossed beside his hip. His face is hidden in the shadows of the vehicle.

I was raised by the head of the Las Vegas mafia, the capo. I grew up around guns and violence, so I know when a man is armed. It's the way he holds himself, the warning shimmering around him like a dark halo.

This man is armed and extremely dangerous.

Every muscle in my body tenses. My mind still swims in thick water, because I must have been drugged. *He* drugged me, this faceless man. Why did he take me? It won't be anything good, that's for sure.

Even worse, I suspect this has something to do with my past, with my family. It's messed up that I'd rather be taken by some random psycho. But at least then I'd have a chance of getting away.

"Who are you?" I demand, my voice hoarse from whatever drugs they gave me.

There's a long pause, the weight of his regard as heavy as a finger trailing down my neck.

"Have I really changed that much, bella, that you don't recognize me?"

Hold You Against Me is available now at Amazon.com, iBooks, BarnesAndNoble.com and other retailers.

Other Books by Skye Warren

ABOUT THE AUTHOR

Skye Warren is the New York Times and USA Today Bestselling author of dark contemporary romance. Her books are raw, sexual and perversely romantic.

Sign up for Skye's newsletter:
www.skyewarren.com/newsletter

Like Skye Warren on Facebook:
facebook.com/skyewarren

Join Skye Warren's Dark Room reader group:
skyewarren.com/darkroom

Follow Skye Warren on Twitter:
twitter.com/skye_warren

Visit Skye's website for her current booklist:
www.skyewarren.com

COPYRIGHT

This is a work of fiction. Any resemblance to actual persons, living or dead, business establishments, events or locales is entirely coincidental. All rights reserved. Except for use in a review, the reproduction or use of this work in any part is forbidden without the express written permission of the author.

Made in the USA
Las Vegas, NV
06 May 2024

89615284R00066